WHAT IS GOING ON IN KAMIAH?
"Maybe it's going to be a kidnapping, or it could be a spy network or an international drug ring or who knows? Don't you think it has to be something big?"

"I don't know, Crystal," Megan replied. "Nothing makes sense to me right now. Maybe in the morning things will be clearer. . . ."

CRYSTAL'S PERILOUS RIDE

STEPHEN AND JANET BLY

Cumberland Presbyterian Church
Dyersburg, Tennessee

Chariot Books
DAVID C. COOK PUBLISHING CO.

A Quick Fox Book

Published by Chariot Books, an imprint of David C. Cook Publishing Co.

David C. Cook Publishing Co., Elgin, Illinois 60120
David C. Cook Publishing Co., Weston, Ontario

CRYSTAL'S PERILOUS RIDE
© 1986 by Stephen and Janet Bly

Cover illustration by Paul Turnbaugh
Cover and book design by Chris Patchel

First Printing, 1986
Printed in the United States of America
90 89 88 87   2 3 4 5

Library of Congress Cataloging-in-Publication Data

Bly, Stephen A.
    Crystal's perilous ride.

    (A Quick fox book)
    Summary: Fourteen-year-old Crystal and her friend Megan accompany Crystal's father to Idaho and find themselves investigating a series of strange occurrences in the town involving a gang posing as the community's leading citizens.
    [1. Mystery and detective stories. 2. Idaho—Fiction] I. Bly, Janet. II. Title.
PZ7.B6275Cq 1986   [Fic]   85-27983
ISBN 0-89191-603-2

*To all our friends
on the Camas Prairie*

CONTENTS

1
THE WILD, WILD WASH

CRYSTAL!" MEGAN SCREAMED AND DUCKED BEHIND the large two-toned blue pickup. She reappeared at the rear of the rig twirling a soaking wet towel in her left hand. Hurling it with all her might at the back of Crystal's head, she yelled, "Catch!" Then she ran behind the pickup again.

Crystal spun around, flinging the dripping towel from her long, straight blonde hair. She giggled as she pointed the hose nozzle toward Megan's hiding place.

A drenched, auburn-haired Megan gasped for air. "Time out! Time out!" she called as she collapsed on the ground in mock surrender. Then, she burst into laughter.

"This is some car wash," Crystal began just as another wet towel caught her in the face. She whirled around to the faucet and twisted it to full blast. "Megan Montgomery Fox, I'm really going to get you for that!"

Megan, an inch or two shorter than Crystal, stood her ground. "Crystal LuAnne Blake, you couldn't catch me if a grizzly bear was chasing you!" She waited a full five seconds and then darted toward the road. She stopped suddenly as she spotted a white Jeep turning onto the highway.

Crystal saw it, too, and dropped the hose. "It's those guys! Quick! We can't let them see us like this!"

The two girls dove behind the pickup just as the Jeep cruised by the station. They leaned against each other and breathed a sigh of relief. "Why, Crystal, honey, you look simply ravishing in that early American wet rag!" Megan drawled.

"Well, Megan, dear, I must say that wet blue denim is definitely your color." Crystal sat down on a small bench to rest. "Is this really the only car wash in town?" she asked. She shook her head in disbelief at the old World War II Quonset hut. The building looked every bit as if it had stood the last forty years, unpainted, in the stark northern Idaho weather. "This is like another world—compared to southern California."

Megan jarred her back to business. 'I'll spray the outside, if you'll clean the inside," she suggested.

"Sure," Crystal said. She jumped into the cab before Megan had a chance to try any spraying tricks. As she wiped the dash and seats she noticed her tan arms. For almost two weeks they'd been traveling through the Clearwater National Forest. Crystal had been wearing long-sleeved blouses and a jacket. She hoped she wouldn't lose the tan she had worked most of the summer to achieve.

"We should have worn our bathing suits," she

10

yelled out to her best friend, Megan. "Then we could catch some rays at the same time."

Megan laughed. "Ha! We could catch more than that. Maybe those boys would have stopped by earlier, too."

"Look who's talking," Crystal responded. "Just this morning you said all the guys up here were a bunch of hicks."

Megan aimed the nozzle under the fender to dislodge large hunks of red clay. "Oh, that was when we were stuck back down that little road by those funny rocks. I thought we'd never see civilization again."

"That reminds me. I think I'll write about those rocks for my freshman science project. They're called the Indian Post Office because of all those messages carved on them."

"How do you know about a freshman science project already? Nobody told me."

"From Karla. That's one of the advantages of having an older sister. But she says it's no sweat. Thinking of a subject's the hardest part."

Crystal thought of her sister for the first time in days. Karla was supposed to come on this trip with her and their dad. They'd planned it for a year. However, just days before their departure Karla had learned that she needed to stay home for cheerleading practices.

Dad was gathering research information for the book he was writing. Three weeks ago Crystal had never heard of an Indian woman named

Sacajawea. She'd only faintly known of the early American explorers Lewis and Clark. Now Crystal had just spent a grueling two weeks riding down the same Lolo Trail these people had hiked 180 years ago.

Crystal had talked her dad into letting Megan come. The two girls cooked the meals and cleaned up. Mr. Blake set up camp, chopped the wood, and kept the fires going. The routine was fun, but the girls felt remote at times. Days passed without talking to any other humans. However, they both agreed this beat sitting around home waiting for the first day of school.

"Except I could be there when Patty gets her horse," Crystal remembered with a sigh. All summer long Megan, Crystal, and Patty Devers had dreamed about riding the new horse Patty was to get. "Now, we're twelve hundred miles away."

Crystal caught a glimpse of herself in the rearview mirror. As she did every time she saw her face, she worried about her eyes. Too close together, she thought, and such an ugly gray. She wished they were green, or even brown. She wiped off the doors and steering wheel, then hopped out to help Megan.

"I've got the topic for my 'What Did You Do Last Summer?' essay," Megan began. "The title will be, 'How to Be a Successful Camp Fire Cook.'"

"What are you going to teach them?" Crystal kidded. "How to drop hamburgers in the dirt?"

"Hey, come on. Not everyone can trip over

their own feet. I thought I'd include a recipe for Crystal's Miraculous Oatmeal Chewies. And we sure know it'd be a miracle if anyone could chew one, right?"

Crystal grinned in spite of herself. "And what about Megan's Exploding Baked Potatoes? We could have been killed!"

"How did I know you were supposed to poke holes in the foil and bury those babies in the ashes?" Megan responded.

"I can see the headlines now, 'Russets Rout Rockies!' "

The girls laughed until the tears rolled down their cheeks. "This is more fun than summer camp," Crystal decided, "but definitely not as inspirational." She sobered up a moment. "Remember how we were going to go out in the woods and have a devotional time every day?"

"Yeah, but that was before we realized the woods can be dark and cold and damp, even in the daytime. Maybe we'll do it tonight. We'll be in a motel room. A real bed and everything."

"And real food!" Crystal reminded her. "Dad said when we finished washing the truck we could choose a restaurant. He'll be back from the bank any minute now. Let's check out that phone booth next to the service station. Maybe it will have a phone book."

"Do you have any change to make a call?" Megan asked. "We might need reservations, and it looks like the station's closed."

"Reservations? In a tiny town like Kamiah, Idaho? Besides, the whole place is a reservation. Didn't you see the sign down the road: 'Now entering the Nez Perce Indian Reservation.'"

"That's Kam-ee-eye, not Ka-my-uh," Megan corrected. "Remember what the man at the motel told us?"

"I also recall he told us that Kamiah has 1,500 people, and it's the biggest town in Lewis County. Can you believe that?"

"If it has a pizza place, that's okay with me," Megan replied as they reached the phone booth. "I haven't had pizza in almost fifteen days. I think I'm having withdrawal pains."

Crystal pushed open the rusty phone booth door. She shoved the door closed behind her in hopes a light would switch on. It didn't. She slammed the door several times, but no light. She strained to read the listings in the tattered yellow pages. She creaked open the door to hear Megan.

"I said, did you find a pizza place?" Megan yelled as she ran an oversize purple comb through her shoulder-length curls. Crystal marveled how Megan's curls bounced back after the drenching she'd been through. Crystal's hair fell straight down. A curling iron helped a little, but not for long.

"Are you kidding? There's one in a place called Grangeville and several down in Lewiston. Nothing here."

"How far is Lewiston?" Megan inquired.

14

"Too far for dinner." Crystal handed her the phone book. "Here, see if you can find anything. May I borrow your comb?"

The girls traded places. Crystal walked up the highway a short way to read the billboards. The phone booth stood like a lone sentry between the Quonset hut car wash and the gas station behind her.

Suddenly, a noise startled her. She searched the highway for an explanation. She thought she could see horses coming fast, straight toward her.

Megan stepped out of the booth. "Looks like the only place to eat is a Chinese restaurant called Charlie Oh's. The rest of the . . ."

"Megan, look!" Crystal shouted.

The girls stared. A lead horseman rode bareback. He looked like an Indian. Behind him galloped some horses carrying men dressed like cavalry.

"This reminds me of Disneyland," Crystal whooped.

"Or the mock hanging at Knotts Berry Farm," Megan added.

As the riders approached, the Indian leaped from his mare and jumped behind a barrel marked "Tire Sale" at the station. He aimed a bow and arrow at the others.

"I don't think that's a bona fide Indian," Crystal said a bit nervously, "with that bright red beard. Indians don't have beards, do they?"

Arrows flew around the two men on horseback.

"How do you fake arrows?" Crystal wondered

15

aloud. She felt dazed and dizzy, like in a dream.

"Throw down your weapon and put your hands behind your head," one of the cavalry men ordered. An arrow whizzed a reply, barely missing the man.

A gun discharged. Glass in the phone booth shattered. Both girls sprang back. Megan yelled at Crystal and then ran. Crystal's legs felt like cement. Her mouth froze shut. She stared as Megan rushed back to her. "Come on, Crystal, we've got to get out of here!" Megan grabbed her arm and pulled her across the street. Crystal's legs finally began to pump as they raced towards the motel.

They heard a fierce howl behind them. They didn't look back. Megan shoved Crystal towards their room. Another shot rang out as Megan gasped, "Crystal! Where's the motel key?"

Crystal stammered, "I—I left it in the pickup." Her stomach churned. The battle sounded closer. It was time for action.

Crystal had never sensed such panic and urgency before as they kicked the door. The lock catch plate ripped easily from the fragile door facing. Once inside, the girls threw themselves against the door. Shouts and scuffles echoed from the parking lot. Then, two more shots.

Megan cautiously leaned over to the window, lifted up the curtain, and peeked out. The blood rushed from Crystal's face. "What do you see?" she whispered.

"Wow, one of the officers is lying on the gravel

16

with an arrow plunged right through his neck. Blood's splattered all over his face. He looks . . . dead.''

Crystal couldn't talk. All she could do was run for the bathroom and heave camp hamburgers. She heard a loud, wood-splitting bang from the next room. She staggered back to help Megan hold the door shut. Pressed against the door, they slumped to the floor and sat in silence for a long time.

Finally, Megan asked Crystal for the time. Crystal relaxed enough to glance at her watch. The lighted dial reported 7:00 p.m. Crystal could hardly believe it. They'd been in Kamiah only two hours. "Why isn't Dad back yet?'' she whispered. "The bank closed at six.''

"He probably found somebody else to interview,'' Megan suggested. "Boy, the Kosy Korner Motel sure isn't living up to its name.''

"Megan,'' Crystal said in a shaky voice, "I acted like a zombie out there. Those bullets, and the arrows. Hey, shouldn't we call an ambulance or something? That man out there. . . .''

Megan didn't move. "Let's wait for your dad.'' She hesitated. "I wish my dad was here, too. I'd even appreciate seeing my brother Nick.''

"You did great out there,'' Crystal assured her. "I was the hypnotized one. I couldn't even think clearly enough to get out of the way. I'm always that way when I get scared. How did you manage to get us both over here?'' Crystal hugged Megan as

17

the tears flowed from their eyes.

Megan wiped her eyes. "I don't know. It's like the time Nick was only four, and he fell in the swimming pool. I jumped in and grabbed him without thinking. I guess I get hyper under pressure."

"I'm thankful you do. All I do is panic, freeze up. I wish I were different. Like when I wake up from a bad dream, I want to scream, but I never can. You'd think an intelligent fourteen-year-old could get herself off a street when there's trouble."

"I did pray the whole time," Megan said quietly.

"Did you really?" Crystal looked at her friend.

"Crystal, did you pray, too?" Megan asked.

"Sure. I just cried, 'Help, Lord!' over and over." Crystal hugged her knees close. "Megan, they were just kidding out there, weren't they? It's some kind of act?"

"There's one way to find out," Megan challenged.

"Do you think we should open the door?"

"Maybe we could take another look out the window, first," Megan suggested. "Your turn."

"Me?" Crystal protested.

"You're the closest."

"But I can't. Remember? I'm the one with the weak knees and stomach."

"Okay, I'll do it." Megan assumed her bravest posture and pulled back the flimsy green curtains. "Hey," she yelled. "There's nobody out there!"

Crystal jumped up. "What? No one at all? Not even a body?"

"Nothing. Look for yourself."

"Megan, if this is a trick, this is the grossest . . ."

"No joke, Crystal, honest," Megan assured her.

Crystal gazed all over the parking lot. No signs of a recent battle could be seen anywhere.

"Let's go outside," Megan suggested.

Crystal took a deep breath. They slowly eased the door back. What they saw next made them both gasp.

2
STAMPEDE QUEEN

AN ARROW WEDGED IN THE DOOR VIBRATED LIKE A dead twig on a tree. Crystal pulled it out from between the 1 and the 2 on their number 12 room. "Would you look at the point on this thing? That's what I call sharp."

"It's definitely not rubber! Crystal! We could have been killed. I wish your dad was here. Our luck may run out soon." Megan surveyed the surroundings with care.

"What do you mean, luck? Remember? There's no such thing as luck. God's been watching out for us," Crystal replied.

"Well, we're lucky that the Lord's protecting us. That's more than that cavalry officer can say." Megan walked out to where the man had last been seen.

Crystal searched the bushes and the parking lot area. "There's no trace of that soldier, or anything, just like nothing happened."

"How about some blood?" Megan prompted. "There's got to be some somewhere."

Crystal paused, then bent low to look under some parked cars. "Nope, nothing."

"How about across the street, at the service station? Maybe there's some evidence."

Crystal held up her hands. "No way. I'm not going to look."

"This is weird," Megan insisted. "It's like the movies, like a mystery or something."

"Yeah," Crystal said, "Maybe that was really Captain Kirk and they all beamed back on board the *Enterprise*."

"Be serious, Crystal. Hey, let's go talk to that motel manager. Maybe he knows what's going on."

"Sure, you go ahead. I'll stay here and guard the room," Crystal volunteered. "You know, in case Dad comes back."

"You mean, in case that Indian returns?"

Crystal shrugged and followed Megan to the motel office. No one was there. They knocked at a door marked Manager. They could see through the screen into a kitchen. The manager and a dark-haired woman with creamy white skin sat at a table. A small gray poodle with a pink collar barked at the girls from halfway across the room.

Megan knocked again. The heavyset man pulled a napkin off his lap and stomped to the door. On his way, he turned down a blaring television. He glowered through the screen door right at Crystal. "Now, look here, girly . . ." he began.

"Hi. I'm Crystal Blake," she said quickly, "and this is my friend, Megan. We're in room 12. My dad's in room 11." Crystal tried to flash him her best smile.

21

"Well, what is it? Make it quick. The pork chops are getting cold, my darling Chi Chi's upset, and the Friday night movie's about to start. Kids like you have no idea what it's like in this business. A guy never gets any time to himself. After seven o'clock and we're full up. I finally get a peaceful bite to eat, and someone's griping at the door."

Crystal's face reddened. "We're really sorry to bother you, but we wondered, do you know anything about a cavalry and Indian chase out on the highway?"

"What?"

"Men, on horses, and shooting guns and arrows. They fought right here in your parking lot. Do you know who they were?" Crystal could tell she wasn't getting through. She suddenly felt like a little girl trying to convince a grown-up of her favorite fantasy. Actually, the more she talked about these events, the more incredible they seemed.

"We don't have things like that around here," the manager sputtered. "Most all the Indians are good, decent folks. We haven't had Indian trouble in a hundred years. And we don't have cavalry. We've got a sheriff's department to handle the law."

Megan interrupted. "Crystal and I saw the whole thing. Surely you heard something? Right in front of our room we saw a wounded man. We think he was killed. They might not be real cavalry, but that guy looked bad. But now, everything's disappeared. We're trying to find out what's going on."

"Now listen here, Bleak . . ."

"Blake, Crystal Blake, and I'm Megan."

He turned back to Crystal. "You, Blake, listen up, and listen good. I've lived in Kamiah most all my life. Moved here from Cedar Springs, Arkansas, in 1943. We're a quiet, peaceful community. Things like that just don't happen. I don't know what you're trying to pull, but this isn't no western town like you see in the movies. You're the ones from California, right? You girls on dope? Let me look at your eyes. You smoking grass? We arrest your kind around here."

Crystal and Megan looked at each other. It was the first time in her life Crystal had ever been accused of anything like that. In fact, most of the time the kids at school teased her about her predictable behavior. "Don't expect Miss Goodie to break the rules," they'd joke.

Crystal protested. "No, honest. And we can prove some of it. Come look at our door. I mean, your door. Somebody shot an arrow into it."

The girls jumped back as the man slammed open the screen door. "Where you going, Jake?" the woman called out. Jake didn't answer as the three marched to room 12.

"Here's the arrow," Crystal said. "I pulled it out of the hole in the door." She showed him the exhibits. "Sorry about the lock. We had to break the door in to save ourselves when they chased us."

"All right, you punkers," Jake fumed. "You think

23

you can come barging into our town and bust up the place, then lie your way out of it? I'll have you arrested for destroying private property."

Crystal just stood there, dumbfounded.

Megan tried to reason with Jake. Crystal could tell she was getting angry. "Don't you even care what we've been through? Surely you protect your residents from . . ."

"Listen to me, Bloke."

"Blake! Rhymes with Jake!" Crystal snapped.

"Whatever. When your daddy gets back from the bar, or wherever, you tell him to get right over to see me. He's got some restitution to make. Or else I'm calling the sheriff. Now, I've got better things to do. My Chi Chi's waiting for me. My pork chops are begging to be eaten. And I'll hang your hide if I miss the beginning of that John Wayne movie."

Crystal took a deep breath and tried once more. "But the Indian—he looked strange. He had a bushy red beard. You know any Indians like that?"

"Now there I've got you. When you talk bushy red beards, you're barking up the wrong barber pole. The only man in these parts like that is Lincoln Green. Old Linc's one of the finest men in Lewis County. Been mayor for over ten years. It's a cinch he didn't shoot no cavalry with no arrows. In fact, he's probably still over at the beauty contest at the high school gym, just like everyone else in town. You can see it for yourself on Channel 4."

A female voice broke in from across the parking lot. "Jake Compton! You'd better come, quick!"

"I'll be right there, Chi Chi," he called back. Jake pointed at Crystal. "As for you, Baker . . ."

"Blake!"

"I'll settle up with you later." He stormed away.

"Boy, he sure had it in for you," Megan said when he was out of sight. "What kind of place is this? I think we'd be safer back in the woods with the grizzlies."

"Or on a Los Angeles freeway during rush hour," Crystal added. "Let's call the police ourselves. Maybe someone's reported something. We can back up their story."

"There's no phone in our room, remember?"

"How about the one across the street? You can use that one," Crystal proposed.

"Me?" Megan objected. "Why always me?"

"You are the oldest," Crystal reminded her.

"Only by two days," Megan countered. "Besides, that booth shattered. And who knows if the phone ever worked?"

"Well, we've got to do something," Crystal insisted.

"I'll go," Megan conceded, "if you'll go with me."

Crystal nodded, and they trudged through the shadows. The only movement on the highway was an occasional logging truck.

It took awhile for Crystal to notice. "Megan! Look! There's no phone booth!"

Megan shivered. "This place gives me the creeps. There's not even a bit of glass lying around. Just

25

two bolts sticking out of the cement. Let's get out of here." Megan dashed back across the street.

"Wait, Megan," Crystal called. "We ought to at least get the truck."

"Can you drive it?" Megan said.

"Sure. I learned how last summer on my grandparents' ranch. I feel funny about leaving it here. Besides, in Idaho you can get a license at age fourteen. I only want to get it across the street."

"I don't know, Crystal." Megan hesitated. "It doesn't seem right."

"Listen, the worst thing that could happen is to have a policeman stop us, right? And that's exactly what we'd like to have happen."

"Oh, okay, as long as you tell your dad I wanted no part of it." The girls hopped into the cab. "Crystal, do you suppose we witnessed some kind of joke or hoax?" Megan slammed the heavy door shut and rolled down the window.

"I don't think so," Crystal replied as she fumbled for the key. "That arrow's no stage prop."

Crystal turned the key, and the truck lurched forward. She slammed down on the clutch and jammed her right foot on the brake. The engine died.

"Crystal, I thought you . . ."

Crystal started the pickup again before Megan could finish. They catapulted out of the car wash and onto the highway. "I think I'll walk," Megan said with no trace of a smile.

Crystal kept going. She hit the accelerator as

they flew across the deserted state highway. She hit the brake. The pickup died again, and she let the blue rig coast to a parking place. "See? No sweat." Crystal took out the keys and jumped down."

"No sweat?" Meagan moaned. "I was about to pray that the Indian would come back and save me from a sure and swift death. Where did you say you learned to drive?"

"At my granddad's. He lives in the San Joaquin Valley. Of course, he only let me drive the riding lawn mower," Crystal admitted.

Megan rushed for the safety of their motel room. They propped the door shut. "How come that manager was so down on us?" Megan questioned again. "It's really bothering me. Do we look like we're wild, or something?"

Crystal walked over to the full-length mirror and examined herself. "We're very grubby looking, but not wild." Crystal also thought she looked a little tiny bit fat. "If I could only take some from there and put it . . ." she mumbled.

Megan intruded on Crystal's thoughts. "What kind of impression do we give?"

Crystal turned to her friend. "I'd say we are . . . that we look . . . my word for it is rustically hydrobeautiful."

"What is that?"

Crystal laughed. "It means, we're wet and grubby looking."

"Don't you think we should go find your dad?"

"I suppose, but he's sure to be here any minute. If we go off, we'll miss him. Let's change our clothes and then decide. At least then we'll only look rustic."

Megan switched on the TV. "You going to watch that John Wayne movie?" Crystal teased.

"No, I wondered if that beauty contest was still showing."

"Oh, you want to scout out the competition, huh?" Crystal joked as Megan threw a pillow. They both stretched out on the queen-sized bed.

"How can Kamiah possibly have a TV station?" Crystal mused.

"It's probably one of those cable hookups, with a free channel for the time and temperature and local happenings. They could videotape the pageant."

"That's sure a fuzzy picture. Can't you get some of the red out?"

Megan sat up. "Shhh, listen. An announcer's saying something."

"Folks, there's been a slight delay. While we're working on some technicalities, let me remind you all to support the activities of the Kamiah Pioneer Days."

Crystal tried to adjust the picture.

"In the morning will be the pancake breakfast, sponsored by American Legion Post 75. Then, the big parade. Over one hundred entries, and for the first time since 1939, we'll feature the University of Idaho Vandal Marching Band.

"In the afternoon it's out to the Kirkland Ranch for the rodeo. Saturday night we'll hear from Jimmy Riggins and his band from Spokane, plus the giant talent show.

"Wait a minute, folks, I think we're ready to continue. Here's Bill Williams, our high school principal."

"Thanks, Lonnie. It seems there's been a slight mix-up with our contestants. Number six, Suzy Ann Walters, wasn't really Suzy Ann Walters. I mean, Mayor Green, would you please explain what happened?"

"Actually, Bill, it's still a bit confusing. As it looks now, there are two Suzy Anns here tonight. One's our own Suzy Ann from Kamiah High. But there's another Suzy Ann Walters who says she's from Preston. The amazing thing is, this Suzy Ann looks so much like our own Suzy Ann. Apparently, she crashed the contest, so to speak."

Crystal kept staring at the mayor, trying to get a clear view with the blurred picture. Suddenly, Megan said what Crystal had been thinking. "That's him! That's the man we saw dressed like an Indian. The beard's exactly the same."

"Thanks, mayor. Sorry for the delay. Now the real Suzy Ann Walters of Kamiah will perform a baton routine."

"Are we sure? Does he look *exactly* the same?" Crystal prodded.

"Sure it's him. Look at him, Crystal, the build and everything."

"Somehow the guy we saw was a little heavier, or maybe shorter," Crystal persisted. "But he looks enough like him to be his brother."

"Anyway," Megan reasoned, "we know he's there at the pageant. He couldn't be two places at once."

"On the other hand," Crystal added, "if they taped the show, it could have been much earlier. Maybe there was time."

"And now, Mayor Green will announce tonight's winner."

"Thanks, Bill. This has been some exciting contest. Our judges this year have been Miss Wallace, the librarian; Mr. Brooke, the bank manager; and myself. Now, the name of the first runner-up is none other than . . ."

"Crystal! Don't you think that's him?"

"Miss Angel Green!"

"No, the guy we saw was younger. The mayor's got some gray in that red beard."

"Oh, thanks, Daddy, I mean, Mr. Mayor."

"Maybe it's just our reception," Megan stated.

"With a teen-aged daughter that looks like her?" Crystal laughed. "No way, that gray hair's real."

"And now, the moment we've all been waiting for. Reigning as Queen of the Kamiah Pioneer Days will be Miss Suzy Ann Walters!"

"Maybe you're right, Crystal." Megan squinted her eyes. "He doesn't look mean enough."

Crystal doubled her pillow and sat on it. "How could a small town have two people who look so much alike?"

"Congratulations, Suzy. Hey, it's great to hear your plans for cosmetology school. Be sure to pick up your scholarship prize right after the Suicide Run at the rodeo. It will be up at the judge's platform."

"Let's go find Dad," Crystal announced.

"I'm right behind you," Megan assured her.

"This has been a delayed broadcast of the Pioneer Days Queen Contest from the Kubs gymnasium. This showing was made possible by Terry's Tack and Tackle Shop and the Kosy Korner Motel, where rest and relaxation are the rule, not the exception."

Crystal turned off the set.

"What happened to this door?"

The startled girls turned to stare at Mr. Blake.

"Dad! Wow, are we glad to see you," Crystal cheered. "You'd better sit down. Have we got a story!"

"Don't tell me you drove the pickup right into the motel room."

Megan quickly chimed in, "No, but I had nothing to do with that, and for a minute there . . ."

Crystal interrupted. "Dad, the weirdest things have happened since you left."

"Well, I have a weird story or two of my own. You'll never believe what happened down at the bank."

3

A SONG AND A DANCE

MATTHEW BLAKE PULLED OFF HIS BROWN Stetson. He loomed like an old west gunslinger before the battered door. He pushed the door against the frame with his boot. The girls barraged him with information before he reached a chair.

"Dad, there was an Indian . . ."

"And, cavalry, don't forget the guns . . ."

"Oh, and bullets whizzed by, and the phone booth smashed . . ."

"Whoa, girls," Mr. Blake said. "Let's start all over. Now, when I left you two, you were washing the pickup, and your biggest worry, as I recall, was how to get the attention of a couple of boys in a white Jeep. From there, one at a time, please."

He listened with intense interest as the girls spilled out their experience. He shook his head and then turned to Crystal. "So, Megan saved you by pulling you across the street?"

Megan looked down at her shoes. "Actually, I was as scared as Crystal. It's just that I go wild in tense situations."

"Yeah, Dad, remember that time I was in the

Sunday school Christmas program? I had only one line: 'Oh, Mother, what will we do for food on Christmas?' All I managed was 'oh—oh—oh.' The same's true in sports. I make the team, but when a game arrives, it's freeze city. Like that time I stood stiff as a board while the winning volleyball point bounced right in front of me. That was me all over again, standing in the highway."

All three turned their heads as the door swung open. Jake Compton, the motel manager, stood there. "Lake? Mr. Lake? Are you back?"

"Yes, Mr. Compton, I'm Matthew Blake. What can I do for you?"

"You could start by keeping better watch of those girls. While you were out they got to horsing around and busted my door. I could call the sheriff, but if you promise to pay for the damage, I won't let it go no further." Jake seemed in a hurry.

"Of course, I'll be glad to pay, if that's fair," Mr. Blake answered. "But, I do believe the girls' story."

Jake visibly stiffened. "You calling me a liar?"

"No, I'm sure not. I'm just saying I have no reason to disbelieve these girls. I've known them a long time. They've never made up tales before." Mr. Blake unfolded his arms. "Say, do you have a western show or some kind of skits during Pioneer Days? You know, shoot-'em-ups for the tourists?"

"We ain't had no shooting in this town since Nate Tucker's wife took after him with a rifle. Luckily, she didn't know how to aim the thing. That was back in '49."

"I'm talking about plays or pageants," Mr. Blake urged.

"We don't have anything but the talent show on Saturday night, and the parade, of course. Now, over in Lewiston they have a pageant. Me and Chi Chi, that's my darling wife, we go over there every year. Back in '55 she played the part of Sacajawea. Don't suppose you city people ever heard of her."

They all laughed. Mr. Blake explained. "That's why we're here in Idaho. I'm writing a book about Lewis and Clark."

"No kidding? You're a writer? How about that? Wait until I tell Chi Chi. She'll want your autograph. Uh, what do you write?"

"Mostly inspirational books about people, biographies, historical novels, that sort of thing."

"Ain't that nice. I sure had you pegged wrong. But I was hoping you wrote some of those romances. Chi Chi loves them."

"I'm afraid that's not my style. Now, as I was saying, do you ever get practical jokers around Pioneer Days?"

"Not like you mean. This is just a little river town. The only time we're this crowded is rodeo week, and the first week of elk hunting season." Jake glanced down at his watch. "I'll be down to fix this door in the morning. Maybe you could push that table against it for tonight?"

Mr. Blake pointed towards town. "Could you tell us where to find the police?"

"As a matter of fact, Sergeant Kingman usually

stops by Charlie Oh's this time of night for dinner. If you hurry, you might catch him. . . . Okay, Blakely, we'll settle your account in the morning." Jake turned to go and then stopped. "Say, if you eat at Charlie Oh's, be sure to try his Oriental Delight #3. It's the best meal north of the Salmon River."

After he left, Mr. Blake said, "Ladies, we've got several problems. First, something odd's going on, and we've got to find out why. Second, I think you'd better take my room. You can't stay in here with the door like this. And third, I'm hungry."

"But, Dad," Crystal interjected, "you never did tell us what happened at the bank. How come you took so long?"

"For one thing, I had a long visit with a man by the name of Jedediah Sorensen. He's a fourth-generation native whose family arrived here before the 1860 gold rush. He's a preacher from across the prairie, in a small town called Winchester. He and his grandson came for Pioneer Days. He gave me an idea for another book. So I'll be talking to him again."

"What about the bank?" Megan repeated.

"I got to the bank just before closing time to cash a traveler's check. Rev. Sorensen stood right ahead of me. All of a sudden there was a great commotion at the bank's front door. Two men walked in wearing dark suits, black shirts, dark glasses, and white ties. One stayed at the front door; the other walked to the back. A second later, a balding man with horn-rimmed glasses entered. Rev. Sorensen remarked that he looked like Mr. Brooke, the bank manager.

"Behind him a man also dressed in black with a white tie walked in. He carried a violin case. He shoved the case into the bald man's back, pushing him along. Then the man with the violin case shouted, 'Don't anyone move.' No one did."

Crystal's eyes widened. "Wow! Just like in the old gangster days. What happened next?"

"The bank manager sauntered over to a teller. The man with the case yelled, 'Tell her what I told you.' The man cleared his throat, and we all strained to hear him. He whispered something. The teller looked surprised. She asked him to repeat his request. This time we all heard him. 'I'd like change for a dollar, please,' he said.

"The teller giggled. Everyone looked around at each other. Some were puzzled. Others were nervous, wondering what would these nuts do next. Then the men in black suits broke into friendly grins. The three of them walked over to the middle of the lobby. The one with the case flipped a toggle switch and some music played. It was the theme from that old movie, 'It's a Mad, Mad, Mad, Mad World.' The men sang and tap-danced right out the front door. Everyone applauded as the bald man left, too. They drove off in a green van."

"How weird!" Crystal exclaimed. "At least your encounter wasn't as gory as ours. What did everybody think about it?"

Mr. Blake walked to the window and looked out briefly. "Well, Jed Sorensen got to talking to me about strange happenings he remembered from the old days in this part of the country. We finished our banking and talked to the teller. She claimed the bald man was not Mr. Brooke, the bank manager. She said he just looked like him. It didn't bother her except for the fact that the gang left their change." He chuckled, "Now her books won't balance."

Crystal jumped up. "The Indian—mayor, the two Suzy Anns at the beauty contest, and now a look-alike bank manager. Do you suppose they tie together in some way? Could our cavalry and Indian episode have been all an act, too? If so, why?"

Mr. Blake put his hand on her shoulder. "Calm down, Crystal. This is a big weekend for Kamiah. It's a rodeo celebration. I'm sure someone's having fun, and everything's under control."

"But, Dad," Crystal reflected, "no one seems to know anything about it. Wouldn't the local townspeople be in on these things? On the other hand, this place is so remote. At least, we think it is. Do you suppose people do crazy things like this when they're so isolated? Maybe they're all in it together to make visitors look foolish or something."

"Crystal, " Mr. Blake admonished, "let's don't jump to any quick judgments. Besides, everybody looks strange to somebody else. Remember when we stood and stared in Times Square that Saturday night a few years ago?"

"Yeah," Crystal said, "we thought those New York people were really weird. Then we realized they were looking at us in the same way."

Mr. Blake took charge. "Okay, this is enough talking. We've got to get some dinner and report these incidents. You girls move your gear to my room. I'll work on making some kind of temporary lock to keep out the alley cats and cold canyon breezes."

"Sure, Dad," Crystal agreed, "but first, we both need showers." She noticed her dad's look. "We'll do it in a hurry," she promised as they picked up clothes and suitcases.

"First dibs on the shower," Megan yelled at Crystal from Room 11's bathroom.

"Hey, don't use all the hot water," Crystal wailed. "Even if we don't have to boil it ourselves, it doesn't last forever."

Megan stuck her head out. "This is going to be the world's fastest shower. I mean it. Time me, and I'll bet you dessert that I can do it in under four minutes."

"And wash your hair, too?" Crystal asked with obvious mistrust.

"And wash my hair, too."

"You're on, Megan Montgomery Fox. There's no way the future homecoming princess of Citrus Valley High can get out of a shower within four minutes."

While the water ran and Megan sang, Crystal sorted through her collection of camp clothes.

Among the wrinkled garments she discovered a neatly folded pair of pink cords and a pink T-shirt with a painted scene of the Cascade Mountains and the claim, "I climbed a volcano." "This will do," she said. "I certainly won't be seeing anyone I know way up here."

"Ta da!" Megan announced, wrapped in her orange beach towel. "I won—only three minutes and forty-seven seconds."

"I'm impressed," Crystal admitted. "How did you do it?"

"It's easy. I've had years of practice because my dad keeps an egg timer in our bathroom and insists we get through before the 'sands of time' run out. Add to that the fact that I'm starved, plus the fact that there's a huge spider in there," Megan explained.

Crystal held up her pink outfit. "What do you think?"

"Sure, why not?" Megan responded as she sorted through her own suitcase.

Crystal sped into the bathroom and got ready in record time, too. Soon they both crowded in front of the tiny bathroom mirror, trying to blow dry their hair. Crystal gasped when she noticed the blue western dress Megan wore. "I thought we were wearing cords," she reminded her.

"Well, I saw this dress, and I didn't know when else I'd get a chance to wear it. I bought it just for this trip, and I doubt I'll ever wear it at home. Anyway, my cords are too tight, all those hamburgers." Megan turned off her drier and shook her auburn curls.

Crystal sighed as she gingerly held a delicate blonde curl in her hand. She knew one wrong move and her hair would straighten. She glanced back at the mirror for one last look and turned off the light. "Let's go," she said. "I'm hungry enough to chew on oatmeal chewies."

"Oh, gag!" Megan choked. "Don't remind me."

Mr. Blake waited for them outside. "I've decided we should walk. Let's see if we can find an Oriental Delight #3 with our names on it."

"Walk?" They both groaned.

They braced themselves against the crisp night air and cut across the highway. Soon they passed a darkened hardware store and crossed an old bridge. Mr. Blake passed the time by giving a history lesson of the area.

"Lewis and Clark traveled down the Clearwater River to the Snake River. That's where the town of Lewiston is today. The Nez Perce Indians assisted them. They considered the Nez Perce to be the most courteous, truthful, and helpful tribe they met on the trip. And they proved good horsemen. You girls are interested in horses. Just across the river spreads Palouse country. That's an Indian word to describe the winds that blow in from the west off the Columbian plateau. That's how their horses got their names: Appaloosas."

Crystal perked up. "Like Patty's new horse."

They could see the lights flashing at Charlie Oh's

just ahead. Mr. Blake shined his flashlight on a sign at the side of the road. Crystal read aloud: "This monument commemorates Lewis and Clark camping here in 1806."

"And look over there," Megan pointed. "This one tells of Rev. James Hays, an Indian born in Kamiah in 1855. It says he was instrumental in leading many of his fellow tribesmen into the Christian faith."

As they walked on, Megan asked, "Mr. Blake, are there a lot of Christians among the Nez Perce Indians today?"

"I'm not sure exactly how many, but there are quite a number. They've had the Bible since the 1830s. A man by the name of Sparelding told them a lot about God. Then the McBeth sisters translated the Bible into their language and taught them to read and write."

"Why would they want to hear about a white man's God?" Crystal inquired. "Weren't they enemies of the whites?"

"Not in the early days. Besides, people of all races crave to know truth. Most people seek to find God. That's what happened to me about thirteen years ago, just after Crystal was born. I was no closer to God than the early nineteenth-century Nez Perce. But I wanted to know him. Now, I believe I do."

Crystal changed the subject. "I wonder what's in an Oriental Delight #3?" Then she felt ashamed. Every time a conversation turned to personal spiritual things, she froze the same as when she got scared. What's the matter with me? she wondered.

Crystal didn't think she wanted to ignore God. "I just choke up, like I'm afraid to let people see me out in the open. Like, what if I said something wrong? What if somebody thought what I believe is dumb? I've never been able to talk about God, or talk to God, like Karla, or Megan," she mused as her dad continued to talk.

Once Crystal had watched her sister, Karla, give a testimony in front of a huge audience. She'd listened to Karla explain her faith to her friends, too. The best Crystal could ever do was invite someone to church, or maybe loan a Christian book to a friend.

Dad startled her back to Kamiah, Idaho. "Crystal! Over here!" She had walked right past the entrance to the crowded restaurant.

Charlie Oh's lit up like a neon oasis in an otherwise blacked-out town. Not many of Kamiah's businesses stayed open on a Friday night, even if it was rodeo weekend. The flashing red glow on Charlie Oh's walls produced an eerie look. Crystal half expected to find a sword-wielding Chinese warrior greet them at the door. Instead, a swarm of people waited to be seated.

"Are you going to call Mom and Karla tonight?" Crystal asked her dad.

"Yes, I suppose so, why?"

"I just wondered. Do you think I could ever be like Karla? You know, so outgoing and . . ."

Megan broke in. "Who needs it? With all your natural innate rustic hydrobeauty." Crystal shoved Megan into a potted plant as Mr. Blake looked mystified.

Megan looked over a bamboo barrier and watched some small children eat their meal. "I hope they have plenty of egg fu yung," she commented.

"I hope we get plenty of Delight," Crystal added.

Mr. Blake smiled at the girls, then looked across the room. "You never know what kind of delight could be just around the corner," he remarked. "Even at a place like Charlie Oh's."

4

THE REAL DELIGHT
AT CHARLIE OH'S

*I*T SEEMED AS THOUGH THE WHOLE TOWN HAD GATH-
ered at Charlie Oh's that night. The waiting
area inside the front door, no larger than a
walk-in closet, had over a dozen people standing
shoulder to shoulder. Plastic plants hung from
macrame hangers separated those who waited
from those who ate.

The long, narrow, main dining hall was to the
left. Along a row of windows were booths large
enough to seat four to six people. The booths along
the interior wall had scrolled Chinese dividers all
the way to the ceiling, making it impossible to see
who sat next to you. All the walls were covered
with red velvet wallpaper.

Crystal watched the cooks through a small pass
window behind the cash register. They all looked
Chinese.

The waitresses, on the other hand, were definitely Caucasian, although their mid-length black
dresses looked Oriental. "Is it always this packed?"
Mr. Blake asked the hostess.

"No, it's the Pioneer Days crowd," she replied.

"Could you tell me, does a Sergeant Kingman
happen to be here?"

44

"Sure, Larry's here. He's sitting at the end booth to your left. He's alone tonight." She tapped her pencil on the register. "You friends of his? You could double with him and not wait so long."

"Actually, we don't know him at all. But we really do need to talk to him."

"Come on, I'll introduce you." The friendly redhead led them back to the lawman's booth. A darkskinned man with jet black hair greeted her. "Larry, these people are from out of town, and they say they have some business to talk over with you. Mind if they sit at your booth?"

Sergeant Kingman stood to shake Matthew Blake's hand. They introduced themselves, and the sergeant asked, "What can I do for you?"

"First," the hostess interrupted, "do you want a menu?"

"They sure don't, Dixie," Sergeant Kingman insisted. "They'll want the Oriental Delight #3. Isn't that right?" He grinned at them.

Matthew Blake waved his hand. "That's exactly what we want, and I'll have a cup of coffee."

"I'll have root beer," Crystal ordered.

"I'll have your regular tea, of course," Megan said, "and we'd like some chopsticks."

Mr. Blake reported to the sergeant what they'd witnessed the past few hours.

"It's that time of year," Sergeant Kingman sighed. "For fifty-one weeks Kamiah's one of the quietest towns west of the Rockies. Then, Pioneer Days are on, and every crazy from Seattle to Salt

45

Lake hits town." The waitress handed Sergeant Kingman a plate of fortune cookies. He broke one open. "Would you listen to this? 'You should take a long trip soon. It will be good for your health.'" Kingman roared with laughter. "Sounds great to me, effective immediately. However, I'm afraid I've got to survive the next few days first. Thanks for the information, folks. I'll check out those stories right away."

"Sergeant Kingman!" Megan blurted out. "You don't sound very worried, or concerned. This could be something very serious."

"Yes, you're right. Sorry for my lack of enthusiasm, young lady. But in my line of work, you learn to take one thing at a time."

Mr. Blake leaned forward. "Sergeant, do you suppose this is some type of publicity gimmick? Someone out to capture some headlines?"

"Ha!" Kingman almost shouted. "I sure wouldn't pick Kamiah to do it, if I were them. He suddenly stopped. "And then, I have to contend with the oddball over to your right."

The three gazed past Sergeant Kingman. An Oriental man in a red-checkered shirt sat alone. "That man's the spitting image of Charlie Oh, the owner here. Only, he's not Charlie. So, what's he doing here?"

"Maybe he's a relative or something," Crystal suggested.

"Nope. Dixie informed me that he walked in two hours ago, introduced himself as 'Charlie,' then chatted with all the customers and workers, just like Charlie Oh does. About the time everyone got nervous about the whole thing, he plunked himself down and ordered a ten-course dinner. He's been eating ever since. Sure can't arrest a guy for that."

"Did you talk with him? Find out where he's from?" queried Mr. Blake.

"He told me he'd heard all about Charlie's famous food. Says he's from back East, on his way to the Washington-Seattle area." He cracked open another cookie. "By the way, how did you folks happen to wind up in Kamiah?"

"My dad's a writer," Crystal volunteered. "He's here to gather information for a book about Lewis and Clark."

"Is that so? Well, I've read a lot about it, from both sides of the canoe, if you know what I mean. There's always been one thing I've wondered about that trip. Maybe you can tell me, Mr. Blake. How in the world did the whole troupe get along so well with two leaders? Having two bosses sounds as bad as coping with two wives."

Mr. Blake's eyes brightened. "It is amazing. In reality, Meriwether Lewis commanded the expedition, by President Jefferson's choice. Lewis picked Clark as his assistant. But from the very first day the crew called Clark 'captain,' even though he was only a lieutenant. A very amiable team."

Excitement in his voice grew as he recited the details. "Lewis, the logical, determined one, expertly handled the men. Clark, the pioneer, could deal with the Indians, shoot straight, and set up camp in the worst of conditions. They complemented rather than competed with each other. In neither of their journals do you detect the least hint of jealousy or serious disagreement."

"It's a cinch they weren't relatives," Crystal chuckled. Megan nodded agreement.

"Ah," Sergeant Kingman said, "here's Dixie with your Delights, and I'd better be going." Kingman grabbed his hat and stood to his feet, as Dixie passed out the steaming, heaping plates.

Pork chow mein piled high on a mountain of soft noodles. Two large portions of egg fu yung, crisp wonton, fried shrimp, spareribs smothered with a sweet, red pineapple sauce, Chinese-fried vegetables with water chestnuts, and a mound of fluffy white rice completed the spread.

Then, Dixie brought the Delights in separate bowls. A pastry about the size and shape of a Shredded Wheat biscuit sat in a pool of melted butter sauce. Inside the pastry shell was a combination of deep-pit barbecued chicken pieces and a fig and apricot paste. Crystal and Megan dug in with enthusiasm.

They ate in silence for a time, except for an occasional *ah* or *ummm*. Then Crystal looked over at Megan. A slight new tenseness seemed to be in the air. Megan sat a little straighter. Even her manners improved. *Who's she trying to impress?* Crystal wondered.

Crystal stole a few more glances at her friend.

Megan's attention seemed to be straying from the food to something across the room. Crystal followed her gaze.

There he sat . . . the most handsome boy Crystal had ever seen. Blond hair, dark eyes, a smile with dimples. He wore a blue, long-sleeved, yoked western shirt with matching blue Apache scarf. A hat like her dad's sat next to him on the table.

"Megan spotted him and didn't even tell me," Crystal fumed to herself. She put down her chopsticks and wiped her mouth with her napkin. She smiled nonchalantly and tried not to stare at the boy. At the same time she peeked at him sideways while pretending to choose a second helping from the bowls.

"He's definitely not Megan's type," Crystal assured herself. "He's a blond, like me, and looks so mature. Rats!" she said, almost out loud. "Why didn't I wear my new western blouse? And Megan's got on her cute dress. I wish I had some cowboy boots!"

Crystal decided he must be the cutest boy in Idaho. Probably a rodeo star, or the son of a big ranch owner, she thought. Maybe both. I've got to think of some way to meet this guy. Maybe he's riding in the parade. Perhaps I could think of some reason to dash out in front of his horse, and he'd have to save me or something.

I ought to just walk right over there and say, "Hey, cowboy, what are you doing after the parade tomorrow?" After the parade? How about after

49

dinner tonight? She threw out that bold idea. I could just walk by, and pretend to faint, or accidentally knock his hat off. No, that's too obvious. But I've just got to meet him before Megan. . . .

Dixie intruded on her schemes with their fortune cookies and the bill. "It was great, Dixie!" Mr. Blake said, "And what a bargain. Our compliments to the chef and Charlie Oh."

Crystal nearly jumped up out of her seat. "Look at this," she cried, "my fortune says, 'You are about to meet a very important person.' "

"Hey, I won your dessert," Megan countered, "So I get your fortune, too."

A deflated Crystal said, "Oh, I forgot."

Mr. Blake stood to leave. "Sure can't complain about the prices here."

"Or the view," Crystal mumbled. She hated to leave, but she had no choice. She wished she had a mirror for one quick check before they passed in front of the mystery boy's booth. She strolled as calmly as possible to the cash register.

"Hey, Crystal, did you notice that blond boy, the way he looked at me? I think he likes me," Megan confided.

"Huh? What guy? I didn't see anybody look at you." Crystal tried to act aloof.

"Are you blind? Look down there at the hunk with the navy blue scarf." Megan nodded her head.

"What about him?" Crystal bristled.

"Didn't you see him smile at me?"

"You must be kidding. He smiled at me, too."

"Come on, Crystal. You're much too—too," Megan stuttered.

"Too what?" Crystal answered. "Too charming and hydrobeautiful?"

Megan laughed. "Hey, no big. We'll probably never see him again, anyway."

"Oh, I'll see him," Crystal told herself. "In my dreams, I'll bet."

"I say his name's Richard, and he drives a black Camaro," Megan speculated.

"Richard? No, that doesn't fit. His name's Lance, and he rides a Palomino."

"Lance? Crystal, that's awful. His dad's got to be a congressman, at least. And he spends half the year touring the world, and the other half as a ski instructor."

"I've got you there," Crystal asserted. "He rides in rodeos, and his dad owns one of the biggest cattle ranches in Idaho. Megan, you're way off."

"What are you two jabbering about?" Mr. Blake inquired. "You're not still hungry, are you?"

"No way, Dad," Crystal answered. "It's just that we're discussing . . ." her voice trailed off.

"Actually, we're debating," Megan interjected.

"Look, Dad, do us a favor. Look down there at the booth by the window. Now, don't be obvious. See the boy with the blue scarf? Wait until he turns his head. There, now who do you think would make a better couple? He and Megan? Or me? Huh? What do you say?"

"Well, I'll be. . . . Come on, girls, there's only one

way to settle this." To the girls' horror, Mr. Blake walked straight toward the boy's booth. They trailed behind, hoping he wouldn't do anything to embarrass them. Crystal ran her fingers through her hair the best she could and caught Megan doing the same.

For the first time, the girls observed an older man sitting across from the boy. Mr. Blake greeted them. "Rev. Sorensen, how good to see you again. I see you have your grandson with you. Girls, this is the man I met at the bank."

The man rose to his feet. "Glad to meet you, ladies. Shawn and I have been talking about you."

"You have?" both girls echoed.

The blond dream now stood. He was over six feet tall. His shoulders were broad, and his face and neck were bronzed from the summer sun. His eyes sparkled as he reached out his hand to Mr. Blake and then to each of the girls. Crystal thought Megan held his hand too long.

His grasp felt a little rough, but it was warm and strong, and gentle, too. Crystal prayed she wouldn't do something stupid, like sneeze or cough or stammer.

"Yes, I was looking forward to meeting you both in the morning at the pancake breakfast. I really wanted to talk to you," Shawn said.

"You did?" Megan said, calm as could be.

"Both of us?" Crystal sputtered.

"Sure," Shawn continued, as though he didn't notice Crystal's nervous behavior. "Grandpa told me you're from southern California. After living in Riggins, Idaho, all my life, that sure sounds exciting. I hear there are all kinds of fun things to do."

Mr. Blake laughed. "You'll all have plenty of time to visit tomorrow. Right now we've got to go. Nice to meet you, Shawn. See you in the morning, Jed."

The night air was brisk as they stepped outside. "Girls, let's walk down to the police station. Kingman said he'd check out our stories. Maybe he's discovered something by now."

"Oh," said Megan, "can you believe I almost forgot our whole ordeal?"

"Too much has been happening, too fast," agreed Crystal. "I don't think my life will ever be the same."

5

WINNER TAKE ALL

THEY HAD NO PROBLEM FINDING THE SHERIFF'S DE-
partment with the police car parked outside.
Mr. Blake knocked on the door. Sergeant
Kingman's voice called out, "Come on in, it's not
locked."

The three squeezed into an office about the size
of a plane's cockpit. Crystal looked around. One
door led to the volunteer fire department. Signs
informed them that this room served as the Lewis
County Sheriff's substation, the Chamber of Com-
merce office, and the local chapter of the Red
Cross. A map pinned to some corkboard behind the
sergeant's desk revealed the layout of Kamiah and
the whole county. A star marked the town of Nez
Perce, the county seat. Crystal wondered if that
was where most of the Indians lived.

Crystal was cold, even with her jacket. She
crossed her arms and rubbed her hands to try to
warm up.

"I'd invite you to sit down," Kingman began,
"but there's no room for chairs in here."

"That's all right, Sergeant," Mr. Blake said. "We
just thought we'd see if you know anything yet
about those disturbances."

54

Sergeant Kingman leaned back in his chair and put his feet on the corner of his desk. When he talked he moved a pencil in his hand like a pointer. "I investigated the motel. No evidence of violence anywhere. No broken glass. No damaged property, except your motel room door. No dead bodies. I talked to Jake Compton. He's still upset about the whole thing. He doesn't take kindly to intrusions in his routine.

"I also talked to Oscar, who runs the service station. He said they ran out of gas by 5:30. No one around after that. The Johnsons, who live behind the motel, are up on the St. Joe someplace, fishing. They always scoot away during Pioneer Days. No other motel guests reported anything. They must have been at the beauty contest or at Charlie Oh's."

Crystal jammed her hands into her pockets. "It's hard to know whether to believe us, isn't it?"

"It's not a question of believing. Unless I find some evidence of a crime committed, what can I do? Here, Mr. Blake, fill out this report for me. Then, we'll go from there."

"Evidence? How about the phone booth?" Megan reminded him. "Something as big as that can't completely disappear. Isn't that an indication of at least a theft?"

"I called McClinton at the phone company. He told me his men from Orofino removed that booth several weeks ago. They're waiting for a replacement from Boise. He claims no booth should have been there," Sergeant Kingman explained.

Crystal and Megan looked at each other. "But we both stood right in it!" Crystal's skin crawled with goose bumps. It made her think of the time she saw a bear in their backyard in southern California. Later, they found out someone had captured a cub in Los Padres National Forest and smuggled it into town. It got loose and wandered down their alley. Meanwhile, Crystal suffered some scoldings and a swat on the bottom before anyone believed her. She was relieved that this time Megan had been with her, and her dad had witnessed some strange things, too.

The phone rang. While Sergeant Kingman answered it, Mr. Blake asked the girls some questions for the report. "Give me a physical description of the men involved in the chase."

"The Indian was about five ten, had bushy red hair and beard, and was somewhat old—you know, about thirty-five or forty," Megan offered.

"He wore buckskin pants and shirt, and those long moccasins that lace up your leg," Crystal added.

"How about the other two?" Mr. Blake prompted.

"I don't know—I mean, we didn't have much time to look," Megan explained.

"They both had medium builds, and one of them wore a mustache," Crystal said.

"Which one had the mustache?"

"The one that didn't have an arrow stuck in him," Megan concluded.

"Watch it, Megan," Crystal warned, "or I may lose my Delight."

The sergeant hung up and turned back to them. "Now, if you're through with that report. . . ."

"That call had something to do with our case, didn't it?" Megan pried.

"Your case?" Kingman frowned. "Listen, young lady, some things are private."

"But, Sergeant, we're the ones who almost got killed! Surely we have a right. . . ."

"Megan," Mr. Blake cautioned, "The sergeant's right."

"That's okay," Kingman relented. "I'm a little edgy tonight. That was McClinton at the phone company. He says an old booth was stolen from him last night. But before you get any ideas, that happens a lot around here. The last time, we discovered one in the middle of Miss Mangini's freshman English class. Just harmless pranks."

"It's against the law to steal a phone booth, isn't it?" Crystal insisted.

"True. However, Orofino is in Clearwater County. That's not my department."

"But surely you can do something?" Megan stopped and toned down her voice. "Can't you?"

"Like what? Arrest a girl for crashing a contest? Jail a man because he looks like someone else? Handcuff some guys for singing and dancing in the bank? Lock up someone for impersonating the cavalry?"

"Hey, how about the arrow?" Crystal asked. "It

barely missed us. Couldn't you trace the markings to the particular tribe, or company?"

Sergeant Kingman shook his head. "Indians in these parts have't used arrows for weapons in over a hundred years. We sure didn't fight General Howard with bows. And too much needless time and energy would be needed to trace the owner or maker. The name next to the nock probably says 'Made in Taiwan.' And I suppose you've been careful about fingerprints?"

Megan hit her fist on the counter. "Good grief! We never thought . . . all those years of reading mysteries, and here I go and blow it first thing."

"Besides," Sergeant Kingman continued, "it's probably a cheap target arrow that you could buy in any supermarket in the state." He scanned the report Mr. Blake handed him.

Mr. Blake cleared his throat. "Sergeant, you mentioned 'we' fought against General Howard. Does that make you a Nez Perce Indian?"

"Full blooded."

"Was your family raised around here?" Mr. Blake asked.

"Yep, over near Craigmont. Grandpa was born down in Oklahoma. They moved us nontreaty Indians here after the surrender at Bear Paw Mountain. Before that, my family roots were in the Wallona Valley of Oregon. However, that was a long time ago."

"Any chance I could meet some of the Nez Perce leaders to ask them about their traditions and

58

such? Might be just what I need for my book."

"No problem, after this weekend, that is. If you don't mind driving over to Lapwai."

Mr. Blake and the Sergeant continued to discuss early Idaho history as Megan flipped through some "Wanted" handbills. Crystal leaned against the rough-cut cedar windowsill. She racked her mind for some explanation of all the day's events. Why would anyone go to so much trouble? Maybe they were trying to get a lot of attention, or they wanted people to get so accustomed to the weird behavior that they could pull off something, and no one would suspect. But what? Robbery? The whole town didn't look worth that much. Murder? But who? or, maybe . . .

"I've got it!" Crystal blurted. "All these episodes are building up to a kidnapping. Somebody famous or wealthy will be nabbed, and everyone will assume it's a joke."

"That's an interesting theory," Mr. Blake said.

"Well, I had a few, too," Megan admitted. "How about alien monsters from outer space who can change into humans? Or thieves waiting to hijack the train at high noon?"

"Oh, Megan," Crystal sighed, "be serious."

"You're out of luck with that last one," the sergeant responded. "No trains here in Kamiah. Personally, I like the alien monster idea. It actually makes more sense. Let's hope they're amiable aliens."

Mr. Blake held open the door. "Okay, girls, we'd

59

better let Sergeant Kingman tend to his business."

As they walked back to the Kosy Korner, Crystal lagged behind the other two. The stars looked as bright here as in the mountains. The sky appeared so deep, so vast, so permanent. She felt like a little bug on an immense ball, scurrying around in circles. Compared to the tree-covered silhouette of the mountains, the pounding current of the Clearwater, and the thousands of stars above, Crystal felt insignificant.

She hurried her pace. "Dad, what's that psalm about the sun and the stars and God's majesty?"

Mr. Blake paused to think. "Psalm 8, I believe. 'O Lord, our Lord, How majestic is Thy name in all the earth, Who hast displayed Thy splendor above the heavens!'"

"And that other part." Crystal searched her memory. "When I consider Thy heavens, the work of Thy fingers, The moon and the stars, which Thou hast ordained; What is man, that Thou dost take thought of him? And the son of man, that Thou dost care for him? Yet Thou hast made him a little lower than God, and dost crown him with glory and majesty!'"

"It makes you stop and think, doesn't it?" Mr. Blake reflected.

"I'm impressed," Megan said. "When did you learn so much Scripture, Crystal?"

"One year we all memorized a whole chapter, the kids in my youth group. I picked out that one. But now I forget how it starts."

"Maybe that's why God created the stars," Megan pondered, "to help us keep our perspective."

"Yeah, can you imagine how simple and puny our little mystery must seem in comparison with all that?" Crystal swept her hand across the darkened sky.

Both girls hugged themselves to ward off the chill. "Crystal," Megan began, "if there was a kidnapping, how or who do you suppose. . . ."

"Maybe it's a kidnapping, or it could be a spy network or an international drug ring or who knows? Don't you think it has to be something big?"

"I don't know. Nothing makes sense to me right now. But, think of it; if we could somehow expose their plot, imagine the headlines. We might get invited to talk shows and do magazine interviews. I can see it now, 'Megan Montgomery Fox Tells Her Story!' On the cover of *People* or *Seventeen*."

"You've got a bigger imagination than I do, Megan." Crystal reflected on the day. Talk about overload—mountains and mysteries and men. Well, Shawn was almost a man. She could hardly wait until morning. They'd have breakfast together and finally get to talk.

"I've got to do something with my hair," she murmured. "And I'd better wash my good blouse. I wonder if the iron will work this time? Maybe Shawn can help us with the mystery. I'd like that." She smiled to herself.

"Crystal, come on," Mr. Blake shouted. "We're about to lose you."

She caught up with them. "Dad, I've been thinking. Something could happen at the parade tomorrow. It seems like a logical time. I'd better bring my camera along, just in case."

"If we go to the parade," he cautioned.

"What do you mean, if?"

"We did come up here for my book, remember? If I get a chance for an interview, we may have to miss the festivities. We're not really here on vacation."

"Dad," Crystal lamented, "we can't be gone when these characters, whoever they are, have their showdown." She wasn't sure if she'd really miss the parade or Shawn more.

Megan's face brightened. "I've got an idea. Why can't Crystal stay here to take pictures of the parade? The rest of us can go for the interviews."

"The rest of you?" Crystal repeated.

"Sure. Your dad and I . . . and Rev. Sorensen and Shawn, of course."

"Wait a minute! That's not what I meant. Besides, what would Doug Taylor think?" Crystal hoped that bringing up Doug's name would get Megan's mind on home.

Megan yawned. "He's a long ways away, and we're just friends. That makes him a distant acquaintance."

"That's not what you said in that letter," Crystal teased.

"Did you snoop in my mail, Crystal LuAnne Blake? Just for that, I'll read your diary."

"You wouldn't."

"I would, too, out loud, over the intercom at school."

"I'd die," Crystal groaned.

"Oh yeah?" Megan said with interest. "Is it that juicy?"

"Juicy! It's so boring I'd die of embarassment."

"Yours, too, huh?" Megan replied.

"Why do we keep diaries, anyway?" Crystal asked.

"Because we don't have anything else to do. If we ever had any real adventures, we'd be too busy to write," Megan philosophized.

When they reached the Kosy Korner Motel, Megan noticed that the "er" in the neon sign was burned out. "The Kosy Korn . . . what a name."

Crystal started to laugh, but she was suddenly exhausted. They said good night to Mr. Blake and entered Room 11.

Crystal propped an extra pillow under her head and waited for Megan to finish getting ready for bed. Across the room she examined a picture of a large gray horse on the wall. A girl about ten straddled the western saddle. Crystal suddenly thought of her friend Patty back home with her new horse. "That's the only thing that could have made this summer better," she said, "if I could have learned to ride." She smiled. "Maybe I'll ask Shawn to teach me. I'm sure he knows how."

Megan flipped off the light. The outside light filtered through the thin curtains of their window as Megan jumped into bed. "Do you think he's a Christian?" she ventured.

"Who?" asked Crystal.

"Shawn, of course. I would guess he is."

"Why's that?"

"Well, his grandfather's a preacher," Megan countered.

"I know, but people have to believe on their own. My dad's being a Christian doesn't make me one."

"That's true, but I still think he is."

"How come?" Crystal was trying to stay awake.

"Because he has such a warm, sincere smile."

"Maybe so," Crystal whispered. She began to dream someone was shaking her.

"Wake up, Crystal, we've got to talk about it."

"Huh? What?" Crystal shot up.

"What are we going to do about Shawn? We're going to be here such a short time, I guess we'll have to take turns, right?"

"I don't know," Crystal replied with uncertainty. "I mean, it's not like sharing a beach towel."

"I've got it," Megan exclaimed. "Let's find out how old he is. If he's closer to your age, then you can sit and talk with him all the time. If he's closer to my age, then I will."

Crystal scratched her head. "Wait a minute, we're two days apart, right?"

"Yeah, my birthday's on June 14th, and yours is June 16th."

"Then I don't have a chance. It's a cinch he's not younger than us."

"Oh, rats, you figured that one out already. You're harder to fool than my little brother."

"What if we forget about the years?" Crystal offered. "Let's find out what day and month his birthday's on, and go from there."

"That sounds fair. Anyway, we'd better both be prepared for the fact that someone as good looking as he is already has a girl friend."

Crystal's heart sank. She'd never considered that possiblity. "Megan, don't even think that. Why, if he does, I'll—I'll. . . ."

"You know good and well you'll freeze up and not say or do anything. Now go to sleep and dream of horses and kidnappings. I'm going to dream of tall, handsome blonds."

Crystal dove at Megan and clobbered her with two pillows. Minutes later the bed had been kicked free of covers and the pillows lost. Mr. Blake banged on the door. "Settle down in there, girls."

They straightened up the bed, pulled their pillows from under it, and tried to sleep. Crystal's whole body stirred with excitement. She could smell an adventure coming. And she hoped that adventure included a blond boy who wore cowboy boots.

6
A MORNING RUN

CRYSTAL'S TRAVEL ALARM RIPPED INTO A GREAT dream. She'd been riding a horse, waving her bright yellow cowgirl hat to screaming fans, and had just thrown a kiss to the boys in the crowd when the piercing buzzer propelled her arm to the bedstand. One eye barely opened. Then, the other. She squinted at the clock.

"Five thirty? Time to get up already?" she moaned.

Megan's muffled voice came from under the covers. "It's not time to get up!"

"Yes it is, you sluggard." Crystal sat on the edge of the bed and adjusted her eyes to the morning gray. "Come on, we're going to run."

"Run? Are you nuts? It's dark out there," Megan noted.

"It's not dark."

"Well, it ought to be dark." Megan raised up on an elbow and peered at her friend. "Why do you want to run?"

"Megan, you told me before we left on this trip that you needed to run every day to stay in shape for the track team, and I should run to train for volleyball. So, let's run." Crystal was now on her feet and stretching her arms and legs.

"We haven't run in two weeks. Why start now? If I know you, Crystal LuAnne Blake, this has nothing to do with track or volleyball."

"We did gorge on a heavy Chinese dinner last night. You've got to admit we both could use some exercise."

"Okay, okay, you win. 'Vanity, vanity, all is vanity.' " Megan laughed while she yawned. "See? I know a Bible verse or two myself."

Crystal pulled on gray sweat pants and a gray and violet sweat shirt while Megan dressed in a bright red jogging suit. After double tying her laces, Crystal headed for the door. "Where shall we run?" she asked.

Megan shrugged. "How about down by the river? Maybe we'll find some kind of trail."

"I don't know . . . I'd rather go to the high school and use their track, if they have one," Crystal suggested.

"Just as long as you count the laps so I can keep sleeping," Megan bargained.

Even though the sun didn't yet crown the summit of the Bitteroot Mountains to the east, there was plenty of light. Crystal knew she could only keep stride with Megan a little while. Megan's powerful legs could easily push past her. Megan always ran straight up, her hands carried low, while Crystal stooped forward and held her hands high.

They were surprised to discover that the school not only had a track, but it was lined with special all-weather material. It was great for running. At the conclusion of their second lap, another runner entered ahead of them. A hooded sweat shirt covered his head. From her position, Crystal couldn't tell his age or what he looked like.

"Let's catch up to that guy," Megan urged.

"I don't think I can go any faster," Crystal gasped. "Remember? You're the track star."

"Oh, sure you can. He's just pacing along." Megan pulled ahead while Crystal struggled to keep up.

Another lap later they closed in on the male runner. "Now, pour it on," Megan called.

Crystal collapsed on the damp grass of the infield. As her chest heaved, she watched Megan catch the runner. She could hear them exchange greetings. The guy flipped down the hood of his sweat shirt, then suddenly sprinted, leaving Megan far behind. As he ran past where Crystal sat, she took a good look at him. He had a neatly trimmed brown mustache, wavy hair, and bulging leg muscles. "Definitely at least eighteen or nineteen," she guessed.

Megan dropped down beside her and held her side a few moments while catching her breath.

"What'd he say, Megan?"

She held her hand up, waiting for the runner to pass after waving. "I said, 'Morning,' and he said,

'Good morning. Nice day to run.' Then he said, 'I'd better quit slouching around and pick up some speed.' That's when he took off."

"That's it?" Crystal replied.

"Yep. But I hear blonds are slower," Megan teased.

"We'd better get back, or we'll be late for breakfast," Crystal advised, ignoring her double jab.

"Do you mean you're all through running?" Megan chided.

Crystal groaned as she stood up.

They had jogged down Main Street to the coffee shop when Crystal asked, "Megan, do you have the motel key?"

"Me! I thought you had it!"

"Oh, no, we're locked out! I can't go to breakfast looking like this!"

"Hey, maybe your dad has another key, or we can get one from the manager. On the other hand, I'm not about to wake him up." Megan peered into the window. "Isn't that your dad at the counter?"

Crystal looked in. "It sure looks like his jacket and the back of his head. But what would he be doing here? We're supposed to have breakfast with the Sorensens."

"Maybe he's getting a cup of coffee. Go on and ask him about the key."

"Go in there? Me? It's full of men and I'm all sweaty and my hair's a mess," Crystal protested.

"Come on, Crys, you're hydrobeautiful."

Crystal strained to get a better glimpse. "I'm not sure that's my dad. Why don't you go in?"

Megan sounded desperate. "Crystal, don't freeze. Just march in. No one will give you a second look."

"Okay, I'll do it, but that means I get first shower," Crystal declared.

The coffee shop smelled of bacon frying and coffee perking. Crystal's stomach growled as she marched up to the man in the brown leather jacket. "Dad, do you have the keys to our room?" she said a little louder than she intended.

Crystal's mouth dropped open as the man turned around. He wore a black shirt and clerical collar under the jacket. "A priest!" Crystal yelped to herself. "Sorry," she stammered, "I got the wrong father."

She exited in the midst of clanking dishes and chuckles at the counter. "Megan!" she began, and then saw her dad standing on the sidewalk next to her. "Dad, I've never been so humiliated. Do you have the motel key?"

"Yes, I do. I heard you girls go out, and I decided to jog down by the river. Afterwards I headed to the high school to try to find you. Next time, let me know where you're going."

They strolled back to the motel as Mr. Blake continued, "Did you girls get to see Brian Ketterman warming up at the track?"

"Who's Brian Ketterman?" Crystal asked.

Megan stopped and whirled around. "You mean *THE* Brian Ketterman?"

70

"Who's Brian Ket—?" Crystal asked again.

"That's the one," Mr. Blake reported. "He was zipping around there like the pro he is."

"Who's—" Crystal began once more.

"Brian Ketterman, Crystal," Megan repeated. "The Olympic star, the world record holder in the 440 and 880."

"Oh, that Brian Ketterman," Crystal shrugged.

Megan grabbed Mr. Blake's arm. "Did he have on dark blue running shorts, a gray sweat shirt, and a mustache?"

"Yes," Mr. Blake smiled.

"All right!" Megan screamed. "I just got run off the track by the world's fastest runner! Wait until I tell my coach."

"Big deal," Crystal scoffed, "My dad could run you off the track."

"Sure, but that wouldn't impress my coach," Megan laughed. "Man, oh, man . . . Brian Ketterman. Okay, world, bring on the day!" she cheered. "Isn't it something what a good run can do for you?"

Within the hour both girls, wearing jeans and tennis shoes, were ready for breakfast. Megan wore a blue gingham blouse with a matching blue scarf around her neck. Crystal had chosen her off-white western blouse with red lace trim across the yoke.

"I thought you didn't like that shirt," Mr. Blake commented as they piled into the pickup.

"Oh? Well, you know . . . I mean, it all depends," she hemmed and hawed.

"It all depends on who you expect to see," Megan rejoined. "I can hardly wait to see Shawn and casually mention about running with Brian Ketterman this morning."

When they arrived at the Legion hall, a line stretched out the front door and down the steps for the pancake breakfast. After a long, impatient wait they reached the serving table. A jolly man stood behind a huge grill. "I said, little lady, how many pancakes?"

Crystal had been searching the crowd for Shawn and his grandfather. "Oh, yeah, sure . . . I mean, just a couple, three or four, thank you." She focused on breakfast. She chose several pieces of ham, a scoop of hash browns, and a glass of orange juice. As she juggled her silverware, she looked around again.

Shawn was waving from across the room. Crystal noticed Megan was halfway there. "That rat!" Crystal muttered, as she sped off. Her knife and fork crashed to the floor.

She finally got them picked up and exchanged for fresh ones. "Need some help?" the friendly man with the pancake spatula offered. She shook her head and strolled casually to the table where Megan sat next to Shawn. Her dad and Rev. Sorensen sat across from them. On the other side of Shawn was an active boy of about eight. Mr. Blake motioned for her to sit next to him.

Crystal tapped the little boy's shoulder. "Did you know you can have seconds on pancakes?"

The boy grabbed his plate and shot off to the grill. Crystal slid in next to Shawn. "Crystal!" Megan scowled.

"It's true. They told us while I was up there." Crystal avoided looking at her dad.

"That's a pretty shirt," Shawn said to Crystal.

"Oh, this old thing? Thank you." She thought she heard Megan gag.

"Yes," Megan joined in, "Crystal's a regular megawestern girl. Anyway, as I was saying to Brian Ketterman this morning. . . ."

"Who?" Shawn looked puzzled.

"Brian Ketterman, the Olympic star, right here in Kamiah," Megan explained.

"Really?" Shawn sounded impressed.

"I saw him, too, down at the track," Crystal added.

"Track? What event does Ketterman ski, anyway?" Shawn asked between bites of sausage and eggs.

"Ski?" Megan gasped. "He's a runner. You know, one foot after the other."

"Oh, sorry. Up here we think more of winter Olympics. A runner, huh? I've never gotten into that much." Shawn bit into his stack of pancakes.

"Me either," Crystal agreed quickly. "How boring, just going round and round a circle. What sports are you interested in, Shawn?"

"I've played some football. But rodeo's my main sport. Calf roping—but when I'm eighteen, I hope to ride the broncs."

"Oh?" Crystal tried to stay calm. "How old are you now?"

"I'm fifteen," he answered. "How about you two?"

"I'll be fifteen on my next birthday," Crystal replied.

"Say, Shawn, what month is your birthday?" Megan blurted.

"June," he said, before taking his last bite of pancakes.

"June!" both the girls shouted. "What day?"

"The fifteenth. Why all the excitement?"

"I can't believe it!" Crystal explained. "You see, my birthday's June 16, and Megan's is June 14th. The odds are fantastic."

Megan pushed for more. "Do you know what time of day you were born?"

"Megan Fox, it's a tie. That's all. A pure and simple tie," Crystal persisted.

"Hey, what's going on?" Shawn complained. "I feel like a volleyball, turning my head back and forth!"

"Volleyball," Crystal repeated, "now, there's a good sport." She hoped to change the subject. "Say, are you in the rodeo today?"

"No, not here. I just do junior rodeos. I'm on the high school team."

"They have rodeo teams at your high school?" Megan asked in surprise.

"Sure, we compete all over the state. It's a big deal in this part of the country."

74

"Where did you say you live?" Crystal asked. She hoped she didn't sound too nosy.

"Riggins. That's about an hour south of here. Down in the canyons. It's where the Little Salmon River meets the Salmon River. Lots of white-water rafting there, if you can afford it." Shawn pulled a pen out of his pocket and drew a rough map on the paper tablecloth.

"Rafting," Megan mused. "That sounds more like it. Much more fun than watching a rodeo. That is," she quickly amended, "I've never actually been to one. I'm sure it's got its . . ."

"I love horses," Crystal broke in. "Our friend, Patty Devers, back home is getting one."

"We'll have to go riding sometime," Shawn offered. "Now, how about telling me about southern California? I've never been farther south than Yellowstone. Tell me about the movie stars, the Dodgers, the beach, Disneyland, and whatever else you can think of."

"They film movies right in our own town," Crystal told him.

"Have you ever seen any movie stars?" he quizzed.

"Only from a distance. They rope off the streets, and the actors sit around in a big travel home while they wait their turns. But we go to Dodger Stadium all the time. I love it," Crystal said.

"I like the Dodger dogs best of all," Megan added. "They're a foot long on an onion roll, with all the fixings."

"How far are you from the beach? I've never seen the ocean," Shawn admitted, "except in pictures."

"My house is only twenty-five minutes from Malibu Beach," Megan told him. "You can come visit anytime."

"Look over there, Megan," Crystal pointed. "There's that man who sat in Charlie Oh's last night. Or is it Charlie Oh?"

Megan stared and then said, "How should I know?" She turned to Shawn. "I guess you've heard about the stories going around?"

Shawn rubbed his chin. "I sure have. Real weird."

"That's what I say," Crystal replied and launched into a description of what they'd seen, and their theories.

Megan concluded, "But who up here could be important enough?" She stopped, then sputtered, "Brian Ketterman. Of course. That's what this is all about." She began to talk to Mr. Blake.

"You never know." Shawn turned to Crystal. "Last May I saw Robert Redford and his daughter at the University of Idaho at Moscow. They have a special environmental foundation or something."

"Robert Redford? He'd be worth kidnapping, I think," Crystal pondered. "Is he here in Kamiah?"

"You never know," Shawn answered. "Let's keep our eyes open."

"Megan," Mr. Blake was saying, "Don't talk about kidnapping too loud. It could make people nervous. And you can rule out Brian Ketterman.

He told me he'd be going to Spokane right after his workout." He turned to Crystal. "Jed's been telling me about some Indian leaders he knows from Joseph, Oregon. They're staying at Lapwai this weekend. They'd make great resources for me, and if I miss talking to them now I'd have to follow them over the Wallowa's. Maybe we should skip the local activities and head down the river to Lapwai."

"But, Dad," Crystal pleaded, "couldn't the three of us stay for the parade?"

"And the rodeo!" Shawn chimed in.

Shawn's grandfather spoke up. "Matthew, maybe we could leave the young people for a few hours. We could get our business in Lapwai completed this morning, then meet them at the rodeo later this afternoon. That is, if you think these girls would be safe with Shawn."

"Ha!" Mr. Blake chuckled, "I'd worry more whether Shawn would be safe with the girls."

"Please, Dad, we'd be real careful."

"How will you get out to the rodeo?" Mr. Blake asked.

"Shawn can drive my car," Rev. Sorensen offered.

"That's right!" Megan cried. "They let you have a license at fourteen, don't they?"

Shawn nodded. "I've been driving over a year. And I'm no hot-rodder," he said to Mr. Blake.

"Okay," Mr. Blake laughed. "You three are on your own until we return from Lapwai. Shawn, if these two get too wild, just tie them to a tree."

They waved good-bye to Mr. Blake and Rev. Sorensen in the pickup. *Wow! On my own, twelve hundred miles from home, in the company of a handsome blond.* Aloud Crystal said, "We might even find out some more about our mystery." She concluded silently, *am I ever glad Megan said she didn't care much about rodeos. I'm one step ahead of her.*

"Let's walk over to the grocery store," Shawn suggested. "I'd like some gum or mints. We still have time before the parade begins."

"Are you here in Kamiah just for the rodeo?" Megan asked Shawn.

"That, and to visit my grandfather. He's all alone and likes company."

"Does he have a very big church?"

"Hey, this is Idaho. The town of Winchester's only 343 people. About a quarter of them go to his church."

"Is your dad a preacher, too?" Crystal wanted to know.

"No, he teaches at Salmon River High School, where I go. He's got math, shop, and drama classes. He also coaches some. What does your dad do, Crystal, besides write?"

"That's it. He writes books and articles, and whatever comes along. He also travels and speaks a lot. My mom writes, too," she announced proudly, "when she's not taking care of Allyson, my baby sister."

"My dad works at the Jet Propulsion Laboratory in Pasadena," Megan added. "I don't understand

78

what he does. I think it's sort of a secret."

Shawn sounded thoughtful. "I think I might like to be a preacher someday, like my granddad. I wouldn't mind having a small church like his either."

"Really?" Crystal responded, as they entered the grocery store. "Then, you're a . . ." She couldn't say it. What right did she have to ask him about his religious beliefs? She realized that Shawn was standing there waiting for her to complete her sentence.

Megan broke the silence. "We were wondering if, you know, you're a Christian."

"Hey, sure I am." Shawn answered.

Crystal wondered why it was so hard to ask him a simple question. It somehow connected with all her other fears. Once again she shot up her very familiar prayer, "Lord, help. I don't like being this way."

Shawn selected some gum, and they headed for the checkout counter. Suddenly, the trio was startled by a loud commotion at the front door. People milled around the automatic doors as they opened. One man held bright lights high. Another cradled a video camera, followed by a young girl and a black-haired woman holding a microphone.

"Are they making a movie?" Megan whispered.

"It must be for television, using that type of camera," Shawn surmised. They stepped aside as the crew passed them.

The woman behind the checkout counter leaned

over. "The dark-haired lady's Sara Jorgansen. She's the cable TV manager around here. The girl's Suzy Ann Walters, the new Pioneer Days Queen, I think."

Crystal turned to the woman as she rang up Shawn's purchase. "I thought that girl looked familiar. But what do you mean, you *think* she's Suzy Ann Walters."

"I don't live here in Kamiah. I usually work the Grangeville store. When they need extra help here, like this weekend, I fill in. Most of the workers today are from Grangeville. The regular staff is helping with Pioneer Days." She turned to the next customer. "I'm even running the whole store today! The manager's out to the rodeo already."

They could hear the woman with the mike end her interview. "This is Sara Jorgansen reminding all of you to come to the rodeo and congratulate Suzy Ann in person."

Crystal stared in fascination. For a brief moment she imagined herself interviewing some famous or interesting person. Then loud, piercing wails from police sirens jerked her back to the present.

Crystal, Megan, and Shawn rushed out into the street.

7
THE MOUNTAIN MOMMAS

*T*HE PIONEER DAYS PARADE WAS ABOUT TO BEGIN.
People lined the curbs with lawn chairs and sat
on hoods of cars to watch the procession. Although the sun beat high in the clear skies, the
temperature was mild. Children clutched helium
balloons and plastered their faces with cotton candy. Everyone strained for a glimpse of the first
entrants.

"Oh, no," Crystal cried. "I left my camera in the
truck."

"I've got my camera in the car," Shawn told her.
"Save me a place; I'll be right back."

"You'll miss part of the parade," Crystal said.

"No way," he laughed, "not in Idaho," and he
hurried towards the Legion hall.

"What did he mean by that?" Megan wondered.

"I don't know, but that police car's sure slow
getting here." Crystal tried to peer around a red
balloon that bobbed in front of her.

"Do you really think something's going to happen during the parade?" Megan asked.

"It's a natural. Nobody'd suspect anything out of
the ordinary. They'd think it's part of the show."

"So where will it be? If it's not a kidnapping, could it be a robbery? Like at the bank?" Megan pointed to the community's only financial institution.

"Maybe," Crystal said slowly, "or, perhaps the supermarket. There's always lots of money there."

Megan looked up and down the street. "How about the hardware store? It's the largest building in town. There might be something worth stealing in there, maybe an antique tractor, or a prize turkey." Both the girls broke out in laughter.

Just then Sergeant Kingman drove the police car past them, with siren still blaring. Behind him trailed the volunteer fire department's rig with the city council riding the back platform. Smokey the Bear strolled along behind tossing out candy. Next, a Model T carried Mayor Green. The girls scrutinized him.

"He's not really the one dressed up like the Indian, but there's a striking resemblance," Crystal commented once more.

Then the parade stopped. "I think they're having trouble," Megan said.

"Aha!" Crystal clapped. "This is it. It's going down."

"Going down?" said Megan, perplexed. "What is?"

"About to happen, you know, the big plot, whatever it is."

"The only thing going down is some pride." Shawn's voice startled them. His camera was

82

hanging around his neck. "Would you believe the queen's car ran out of gas? Really. I heard them talking. Her car's on loan from an auto dealer, and they assumed it came complete with gas. Isn't that something? Go two blocks and chug."

"Megan and I've been thinking. If there's going to be a robbery, it would probably be the bank, the supermarket, or that hardware store. What do you think, Shawn?

"I think you're right. The bank's closed today, but with enough diversions I'm sure someone could manage a break-in."

"Let's take turns," Crystal suggested. "I'll watch the hardware. Megan, you guard the supermarket. And, Shawn, how about you looking over the bank?"

"Who's going to watch the parade?" Megan chided.

"We'll all watch the parade. You know what I mean. Anyway, the parade doesn't seem to be going anywhere."

They spotted Sergeant Kingman walking down the parade route carrying a five-gallon gas can. Soon the queen's car rolled by.

Crystal watched Suzy Ann Walters as she sat on the back of the white convertible and waved to the cheering crowd. It seemed like a canned, stilted wave to Crystal. "It must be the kind they teach you in waving school." Crystal chuckled to herself. "She could wave to two million people in New York like that." Crystal tried to think how she'd wave if she were queen, but she could only imagine herself on a horse, not on a car.

"Idaho queens ought to ride horses," she told Shawn.

"I'll agree with you there," Shawn answered.

Megan elbowed her. "Crystal, I don't think that's the same Suzy Ann Walters we just saw in the supermarket."

"I can't really tell. It looks like the same dress. What makes you think so?"

"The girl in the supermarket had chubbier arms. I noticed it right away."

"But this Suzy Ann's not so skinny." Crystal noticed Shawn frown at the put-down. "But she's cute. I mean, we all have our imperfections."

"Oh, yeah? What are your imperfections, Crystal?" Shawn teased.

"Definitely my eyes. Look at the color." She stared straight at Shawn. "See? Boring, dull gray."

"I guess I've never thought much about the color of people's eyes," Shawn admitted.

"You didn't?" Crystal said thoughtfully. She stood up to stretch her legs. "What about you, Megan? Is there something you don't like?"

"My height. I'm only 5'3½", and I wish I was at least 5'5" like Crystal," she reported. "And you, Shawn? What would you like to change?"

Crystal couldn't imagine what it could be. She thought he was perfect.

Shawn watched a float approach. He set his camera and took a picture of it, along with the university marching band. "I'll tell you something I wish I didn't have, my birthmark."

"Where is it?" Megan blurted.

"Megan!" Crystal cried in embarrassment.

"Don't worry, Crystal," Shawn assured her. "It's right here." He rolled up his shirt sleeve high on his upper arm.

"It looks like a burn," Crystal remarked as she studied the round blotch of skin. "Does it hurt?"

"Only my ego." He grinned. "Dad calls it my brand. Says he'll never lose me in a herd of kids. Hey, here come the little leaguers."

Then came a large trailer with a swarm of uniformed Boy Scouts who chanted and cheered. After them marched the Clearwater Valley High School band, two more floats, and the queen and her court from the Cottonwood Buggywhip Days. Just as Crystal wondered what Buggywhip Days was all about, gunfire and explosions shattered the air. She and Megan ducked behind Shawn.

"I hope those are blanks," Crystal called out.

Shawn looked down the street. "It's nothing to worry about. That's the Mountain Mommas. They're in every parade in Idaho and Montana."

Six women with painted faces and western clothes riding horseback—some saddled backwards, shot their way down the street. Two stretched a clothesline between them.

"Usually there's twelve of them," Shawn commented. "They know how to ride those Appaloosas."

All of a sudden, four of the women charged the crowd and broke through to the sidewalk. They leaped from their mounts and plowed into the hardware store, firing all the way.

"This is it!" Crystal hooted.

One of the Mommas emerged from the store with a hangman's noose in one hand, pushing the hardware store owner forward with the other. He held a large gunnysack that had the word MONEY printed on it. The Mommas threatened to hang the man if he didn't hand over the bag. Finally, he threw it at them. The bag burst open, and candy spilled all over the street.

"It's their regular routine," Shawn explained. "They're a northwest legend."

The parade continued with matched pairs. Dozens of teams of double riders wearing twin costumes rode identical horses. Behind them followed the finale, a stagecoach with the league-winning ladies' softball team riding inside.

"That's what you call a deluxe, handmade stagecoach," Shawn exclaimed. "I'll have to get a shot of that out at the rodeo. It plays an important part in the suicide race."

Crystal got ready to leave.

"No, wait, it's not over," Shawn said.

"What do you mean?" Megan asked. "I thought that was the last entry."

"It was. But now they turn around and come back down the street."

"The whole parade?"

"Sure, that way you don't miss anything. The second time through they go much faster."

Shawn was right. Fifteen minutes later, the announcer notified everyone that the carnival gate was opening.

"Shall we go to the carnival?" Megan inquired.

"Sure. The rodeo's not for a few hours." Shawn led the way.

The carnival arena was dusty and very crowded. People of all ages and shapes tried to pack into the short midway. Along the way community service clubs displayed their wares. They sold everything from pies to hamburgers to Indian fry bread. To the southwest, toward the mountains, were the rides and games of skill and chance.

Shawn attempted several times to win some prizes for the girls. He tried the dime toss, the dart throw, and the milk can throw. He finally scored a big win at the ringtoss. He had a choice of two six-packs of cola or a live duck. To Crystal's relief, he picked the cola.

"Here's an event you'll want to try," Shawn challenged.

"What's that?" Crystal asked.

"It's a throwing event. The longest distance wins a $100 gift certificate at Wilson's Western Wear," he responded.

Crystal watched the contestants. "What is that they're throwing?"

He grinned for a moment before answering, "Cow chips."

"What?" squealed Megan.

"Dried cow chips," he explained. "You know . . ."

"We know exactly what it is," Crystal assured him. "We've had our share of those out in the woods."

Shawn led them to another competition. A group of people stood around a circle of bales of hay. Inside the circle loose hay lay a couple feet deep. In the middle of the loose hay was an upright mechanical bull. Shawn bought a ticket and stood in line. "All you have to do is stay on the bull until the bell rings." He handed his camera to Crystal. "If I ride it long enough, take a picture."

When Shawn mounted the black leather bucking machine, he held the rope handle with one hand. The operator of the machine called out, "Novice, intermediate, or pro?"

"Pro!" Shawn shouted, and the man set it for its wildest ride. All the spectators yelled and screamed as Shawn held on. Crystal and Megan cheered the most. A couple times Shawn was kicked up in the air so hard that Crystal knew he'd fly off. But his grip held. He stayed until the buzzer.

"Hey, where you from, cowboy?" the operator hollered.

"Riggins," Shawn shouted back, as he gingerly walked over to the girls.

"All right, folks, you saw it happen," the operator broadcasted. "Ridden by a young wrangler from Riggins way. Now, who's next?"

"You girls want to try?" Shawn asked, half kidding.

"Not me," Megan quickly responded. "I like all my body parts arranged just the way they are."

"Crystal, you like to ride, give it a try. It's fun." Shawn gently shoved her towards the ticket booth.

"Actually, I've never . . . I mean, I want to some-day, but . . . ." Before she knew it, she'd paid for her ticket.

While she waited for an older man to have his turn, Shawn gave her some tips. "Ask for the slow-est speed, just relax, grip tight, and don't fight the motions. Go with them."

Crystal shook as she mounted the mechanical bull. It seemed higher from here than from ring-side. The operator shouted, "Novice, intermediate, or pro?"

Crystal couldn't get the words out. She sat taut, like a statue. "Choose one, lady, it's your poison," the man yelled.

"Intermediate," Shawn yelled out.

Crystal wheeled around in Shawn's direction, just as the machine dropped down. It swung slowly to the left. Then, with one sudden cataclysmic lunge, the machine's rear shot straight into space. Crystal flew into the loose straw. Her head crashed into one of the hay bales. Shawn and Megan helped lift her up.

"Crys, are you okay?" Megan gently prodded.

"Where you from, little lady?" the announcer intoned.

"Er, uh, southern California," Crystal managed.

"Well, folks, Sunny from southern California just broke the record for the longest flight out of Kamiah. The Wright brothers would've been proud of her."

Crystal gritted her teeth as she said, "That was kind of fun."

They walked over to the Ferris wheel. When it was time to load, the man at the gate announced, "Only two in a gondola."

"Maybe Crystal would like to be alone to nurse her bruises," Megan offered.

"But, but . . ."

Before Crystal could finish, Megan grabbed her arm and dragged her toward the open cage. "No use holding up the line. Shawn, I guess you'll have to ride by yourself."

"Oh, boy, this is really great," Crystal griped as they strapped in their seat belts.

"Look at it this way," Megan explained as the Ferris wheel eased to the top. "I may have saved you from possible harm."

"What harm?"

"What if you and Shawn were in one of these cramped gondolas, and he suddenly put his arm around you?"

"Yeah, what if?"

"You'd clam up like a dead fish and mortify yourself."

Megan let out a prolonged scream as the wheel began its descent.

"Did you see the man riding the bucking machine?" Shawn asked them excitedly after the ride.

"When?" Megan replied.

"Just now, from the top of the Ferris wheel, I could see the guy plain as can be. He wore a gray hat and it stayed on the duration. I'm sure it was Ray Pullman. I just know it was."

"Who's that?" Crystal asked for both of them.

"He's last year's All-Around Cowboy at Cheyenne." Shawn tramped back toward the mechanical bull ring. The girls hurried to keep up.

"Was that Ray Pullman?" Shawn asked the operator.

Well, son, I can't say. He didn't tell his name. Come to think of it, he looked like the picture on those boot posters." The man paused and said, "By golly . . . no, no, it couldn't have been him."

"How come?" Shawn pressed.

"Because he called out intermediate. No way would Ray Pullman ride intermediate."

The trio headed for the food booths. "You guys want a corn dog? I'll buy," Megan offered.

"Sure, thanks," Shawn replied. "But the lines are pretty long right now. I'd like to see that deputy sheriff before we leave for the rodeo."

"Me, too," Crystal said. "Maybe we could learn some more."

"I'll brave the line," Megan volunteered. "You two go to the sergeant's office. I'll meet you there."

Crystal couldn't believe her ears. She didn't look back as she walked beside Shawn.

Sergeant Kingman was bent over a pile of papers on his desk when the two walked in. A switchboard behind the desk flashed about two dozen small green lights. Crystal couldn't recall seeing them there the night before.

"Sergeant, do you remember me? Crystal Blake? My dad's the writer."

"Sure do. This your brother, or your fiancé?" the lawman replied.

Crystal blushed. "Neither. This is Shawn Sorensen from Riggins. I was curious whether you'd learned anything new, that is, anything you can tell me," she added.

"No, but you'd be interested to know I've arranged for the Idaho State Highway Patrol to send some cars to patrol the town while I'm out to the rodeo." He smiled. "Someone's got to watch out for the drunks."

"So you're starting to think we might be telling the truth?"

"I never said I didn't believe you. I'm just taking precautions, that's all, precautions."

"But, Sergeant, if a big crime's committed right here in your town, won't you want to be here? All these skits could be leading up to a real setup. The old 'crying wolf one time too many' trick."

"Wait a minute, I've got enough headaches this weekend without your trying to invent some. We've got everything under control. Don't you worry."

"I sure hope so. The Indian and cavalry near the

gas station. The song and dance at the bank. The copycat at Charlie Oh's. An impostor at the beauty contest. Each one of these situations could be potential crime ploys. I'll bet all those businesses hauled in plenty of money, with so many tourists around. That leaves only the supermarket and the hardware store untouched."

"You sure have it all figured out, don't you?" the sergeant marveled.

"Sergeant?" It was Shawn's turn.

"Yes, sir?"

"How long before the parade did Suzy Ann wait? I mean, how long was she stuck in her car?"

"At least an hour. She sure was nervous. She had to pose for pictures the entire time."

Crystal's eyes brightened. "Right before the parade began, someone posing as Suzy Ann was doing a TV interview at the supermarket."

"Wasn't Suzy Ann," Kingman affirmed. "She was with me."

"That leaves only the hardware store. By the way, why were there only six Mountain Mommas this year? There's always been twelve before," Shawn asked.

"Funny thing about that. I got a call about eight this morning saying they couldn't make it this year. Their truck broke an axle in Missoula."

"Well, six of them made it somehow," Crystal repeated.

"I missed that part of the parade. Got a call to investigate a fight on the highway. It was either a false report, or the guilty parties left before I got there."

Crystal's voice began to rise. "You don't suppose those Mountain Mommas were impostors, too?"

"That reminds me, is Ray Pullman in town, Sergeant?"

"Pullman? I hear he's in a hospital in Ogden. Why?"

Shawn shook his head. "This is getting really wild."

"Kids, I'm not saying anything about anything, yet. I'm sorry, but could you run along? I've got a number of phone calls to make." He abruptly dismissed them as he lifted the phone beside the blinking green lights.

They met Megan outside and filled her in on their conversation. "Now we're getting someplace in this case," Megan responded, as they sat on a bench in front of the sheriff's office to eat.

"We?" Sergeant Kingman slammed his door. "Listen here, there's no 'case' as far as you're concerned. And *if* there was, it's strictly police business. I think I can handle my own investigations. By the way, are you going to the rodeo?"

They nodded.

"I need you to deliver a message for me."

"Sergeant Kingman," Crystal protested, "I thought you . . ."

He ignored her and motioned to Shawn to come into the office. When Shawn returned, the girls had finished eating.

"What did he say?" they both asked at once.

"He gave me a note to give to Mr. Kirkland. He owns the ranch where the rodeo's held," Shawn stated coolly.

Crystal held out her hand. "May we see it? Maybe we can hold it up to the light as soon as we get out of town," she suggested.

"I don't know if we should." Megan hesitated.

Shawn laughed and handed the note to Crystal. "Come on, you two, it's not even sealed. Sergeant Kingman let me read it. I suppose you can, too."

They walked to the Legion hall parking lot while Crystal unfolded the paper. "Soooo, the sergeant's coming out to the rodeo later. He wants Kirkland to ask some members of the sheriff's posse to help keep the peace out there. I didn't even know there was such a thing as a posse around anymore."

"They're horsemen who hold honorary positions," Shawn explained. "Mostly they ride with the sheriff for parades."

"Anyway, I'm glad the sheriff's staying in town," Crystal said. "Now we can relax and enjoy the rodeo."

When they reached the car, Megan hopped in the middle of the front seat. "Crystal, you know you get carsick," she answered Crystal's look.

"But I always get sick on the person to my left," she kidded quietly, so Shawn wouldn't hear. She didn't really mind Megan sitting there. After all, she'd spent fifteen minutes alone with Shawn while Megan went for corn dogs.

The drive to the rodeo grounds took them past an old sawmill, across a small valley full of white-faced cattle, and up a red stone canyon wall. Crystal hadn't taken time to look in a mirror since early morning. She tried to peek at the rearview mirror, without seeming to. Her hair was a mess, but she didn't want to comb it right now, not with the window down and the country air refreshing her.

Turning toward Megan and Shawn, she listened as they talked about learning to drive. When they paused, she said, "I hope Sergeant Kingman has plenty of help. He's going to need it."

Shawn steered the car left, down a road marked by a sign and arrow: A. B. Kirkland Ranch—Pioneer Days Rodeo. He half turned to the girls and said with a grin, "You should have seen what the sergeant showed me in his office."

8

THE HOTTEST CHILI
IN LEWIS COUNTY

SHAWN SLOWLY SCANNED THE GREEN HIGH PLAINS
as Crystal watched for some clue in his ex-
pression. She finally broke the silence. "Well,
are you going to tell us or not?"

He grinned again. "I just happen to know that
they've got silent alarms hooked up all over town,"
he reported.

"So that's what all those green lights were."
Crystal felt more at ease.

"Right. If anyone enters one of those buildings, a
light will go on in Sergeant Kingman's office. He'll
be ready to investigate in no time. Meanwhile, the
crook never hears or sees a thing."

"What if the sergeant's out of the office?"
quizzed Crystal.

"He doesn't plan to be. However, he has a buzzer, too—in case he's asleep, or something," Shawn
added.

"So even in Small Town, USA, they use silent
alarms. Those criminals, whoever and whatever
they are, don't stand a chance." Crystal stopped a
moment. "Why aren't we staying in town? We
could watch the alarm for Kingman. After all,

97

we've got some stake in this. We almost lost our scalps." She shuddered at the memory. So much had happened in less than twenty-four hours since the incident at the Kamiah car wash. She had been more excited than she could ever remember. "Not bored," she assured herself, "definitely not bored!"

Shawn maneuvered a second turn down a dirt road. A marker informed them the rodeo was three miles away. Shawn added more details. "The point is, Sergeant Kingman's no dummy. He expects serious trouble. This also means he believes your story. He warned me that the criminals may be armed. He doesn't want us in the way. He's going to radio Nez Perce and Grangeville to see if they can spare a few deputies."

"Why did he tell you all that and not include us?" Megan grumbled.

"Uh . . . because," Shawn replied, "that was man-to-man talk."

"Chauvinists!" Megan scoffed. Shawn laughed.

Shawn's news aroused both excitement and disappointment in Crystal. She cheered to think that the case could break loose at any moment. However, they wouldn't be a part of it. They couldn't even witness the capture.

She imagined Sergeant Kingman kicking in the bank door. Some shots would be fired, and he would dive behind a table. A masked man would sneak up behind him, but someone would warn the lawman. He'd turn, and with a series of kicks and swings, apprehend the gang karate fashion.

All except the leader—he'd be the red-bearded Indian. He'd try to run out the back door. But Crystal would push a potted plant in front of him. He'd trip and crash into the door casing. "That ought to knock him out," Crystal mused.

Crystal would love to return home with some breathless tale of adventure for her friends. "Of course," she told herself, "I could always exaggerate things here and there." But she dismissed that idea. She always got sick to her stomach when she lied.

Crystal stared out the window at a small corral of horses. She studied one gray Appaloosa. For almost six years Crystal had begged for a horse. But the prospect dimmed. At high school she'd need money for clothes, special events, and more clothes. She held out a faint hope that she'd at least get to ride a horse on this trip. Maybe through Shawn somehow. . . .

Megan's voice interrupted her reverie. "Mr. Blake said they used to dig for gold up in those canyons," she told Shawn.

"Yes, that's what brought my great-great Grandpa Sorensen to this region. A hundred-twenty years ago miners flocked by the thousands down this very trail, over the pass to Elk City, Dixie, and Florence. When the gold ran out, most of them left. My family stayed."

They turned down a gravel drive that led to the rodeo grounds entrance. Shawn parked the car in a pasture, and they all piled out.

While Megan and Crystal combed their hair, Shawn sat on the back of the car and surveyed the countryside. They could hear the noise from the arena. Crystal noticed that most of the vehicles in the makeshift lot were pickups with Idaho license plates.

The sun beamed down, and Crystal wished she'd worn a sleeveless shirt. She shaded her eyes for a look into the stands. Then an unpleasant thought struck her. "Shawn, this isn't going to be gory, is it?"

"Gory?" Shawn replied. "Have you ever been to a rodeo?"

"Nooo," she allowed, "but I've wanted to."

"How long have you wanted to go to a rodeo?" Megan whispered to Crystal as they walked to the gate.

"Ever since last night," Crystal whispered back.

Shawn gave them some background. "There is an element of danger in a rodeo. There's a mixture of skill and the luck of the draw. One-ton bulls and kicking horses present a threat. But the risks make victory so sweet. Isn't that the way much of life is?"

"Not if you freeze every time," Crystal muttered.

"What did you say?" Shawn asked.

"Oh, nothing . . . I'm curious if you ever won any trophies."

"Sure," Shawn reported matter-of-factly. "Some silver, some ribbons, but not as many as my sister, Sally."

"You've got a sister?" Megan turned to him. "Why didn't you tell us?"

"You didn't ask," Shawn told her. "Sally's five years older and married. She lives on a ranch near Three Forks, Montana."

"Your sister rides bulls and bucking horses?" Crystal probed.

"She barrel races. It's a timed event. She also used to do some goat roping." Shawn asked a man wearing a rodeo badge where they could find Mr. Kirkland.

"See the booth at the top of the stands? Look for a man in a bright green-checkered shirt, green tie, and white hat and boots. You can't miss him."

They climbed the stairs and quickly found A. B. Kirkland. He also wore a large, gem-studded silver belt buckle that sparkled in the sun.

Shawn greeted him. "Mr. Kirkland? I'm Shawn Sorensen. I've got a note for you from Sergeant Kingman in town."

Mr. Kirkland slapped him on the back. "Say, aren't you the Sorensen boy from Riggins?"

Shawn looked surprised. "Yes, how did you know?"

"You play defensive back for Salmon River, right? Been to the games when you played our team. You're quite a hustler."

"Thank you, sir. Do you know my granddad, Jedediah Sorensen?"

"Sure do. I've had occasion to use his services from time to time," the big man commented. "Why don't you and your gal friends come over to the booth?" He swung open a white wooden door and motioned to them.

They entered the eight-chair booth of A. B. Kirkland. From this vantage point they could see everything, even the parking lot and the countryside beyond the arena.

"Now, what's this about a note?" Kirkland inquired. As he read the letter, his tanned face wrinkled a moment. "Is there some kind of trouble in town?"

"Not yet, anyway," Shawn stated. "There's been some funny business, and the sergeant wants to keep an eye on the town while everyone's out here."

Mr. Kirkland yelled to a man with a badge. They talked in private outside the booth. When he stepped back in, Crystal asked, "Is there any problem not having the officers out here?"

"There's never been any trouble at these things that the boys and I couldn't handle. Just a fistfight or two. You girls from Riggins, too?" he asked.

"No, we're from southern California. I'm Crystal Blake, and this is my friend, Megan Fox. We're traveling with my dad, who's researching a book project."

The rancher looked them over again. "Why don't you all stay up here and watch the show with me?"

They didn't need any more urging. Besides, by now the stands began to overflow. Mr. Kirkland explained the event out in the arena, bull riding.

Then he blared, "Yee—ah! Thataway, Bubba!" He slapped his knee with his white hat. "You see that big, old ugly Brahman bull? That's my Bubba. I raised him since he was a little kicker. Fellow from McCall's trying to ride him."

At that moment, the rider took a spill. He quickly leaped up from the ground and scurried back to the fence while the rodeo clowns diverted the bull.

Crystal thought bull riding seemed like a hard way to make a living. The only ones that looked as though they enjoyed it were the bulls. One rider, his hand caught in the rope, was dragged halfway across the arena. Crystal hoped Shawn wouldn't ride bulls.

As she tried to look somewhere else for a while, she noticed the gaily decorated platform on the other side of the stands. She pointed toward it and asked, "What's that booth down there, Mr. Kirkland? Who are those people?"

Kirkland drew his attention from the arena. "That's the rodeo committee. They pass out the prizes. Now, as I was saying, in bull riding the cowboy must grab a long rope twirled around the bull's middle. He's got to stay on for eight seconds."

Crystal still was interested in the beribboned platform. "Who's on the rodeo committee, Mr. Kirkland?"

Mr. Kirkland turned to Shawn. "This gal's just like my wife. Don't care what's happening in the arena, just watches the people in the crowds. Okay,

103

little lady, I mean, Crystal, on the committee this year is the mayor, Linc Green; and Charlie Oh— he's the grand marshall; Mr. Brooke at the bank; and what's that fella's name at the supermarket? Anyway, he's there. And Turner from the hardware. Of course, Suzy Ann Walters is there, 'cause she's queen. She's going to . . ."

Crystal stood for a better view. "Wait a minute. Green, Oh, Brooke, Walters. That's almost everybody."

"Except for Oscar at the service station," Shawn offered.

"Oscar?" Mr. Kirkland echoed. "That's right! Oscar's up there, too. He's Lion's Club president this year. Why, you all know more about it than I do."

The roar of the crowd turned their attention back to the arena. Another rider fell, and Mr. Kirkland continued his monologue. "Bareback riding's tricky. The cowboy doesn't have any reins to control the horse, yet he must stay on top ten seconds while the animal bucks with all he's worth. It takes a tough man to win. Still, it's not as grueling as the Suicide Run." He stopped to wipe his brow with a green-checkered bandana.

For a few moments Crystal allowed herself to watch the bronc riders. She followed the break from the gate, the twists. She found herself secretly cheering the animals in their struggle to toss their load. But when the cowboy courageously stayed on, she joined the others in applauding horse and human alike.

104

"Are you kids hungry?" Mr. Kirkland asked during a break. "If so, you'd better go down to the concessions before the mobs get there. We cook some pretty special chili you won't want to miss."

Shawn motioned to the girls. "Sounds great to me. Come on, let's get some grub. Those corn dogs were pretty small."

Crystal's mind returned to the rodeo committee. She had a premonition that it was no coincidence that each of them had had a run-in of some sort with the mysterious impostors. She hated to leave her observation vantage point. "How about you guys going for the chili? I'll stay here. I want to talk to Mr. Kirkland about horses."

"Are you sure?" Megan asked, looking surprised.

"Sure I'm sure. Go on, and bring back plenty of hot sauce." Crystal waved them away.

Mr. Kirkland's face lit up. "You like hot chili?"

"Oh, yes," Crystal assured him. "I always get the spiciest salsa when we eat at Mexican restaurants. My whole family teases me."

After Shawn and Megan left, Mr. Kirkland said, "So you like horses? Do you own one?"

Crystal kept one eye on the rodeo committee. "No, but my friend Patty Devers is getting a quarter horse gelding. I'd really like to have one, but we live in the city. It costs a lot to board one in a stable.

Mr. Kirkland pulled off his hat and scratched his head. "Too bad, I think kids miss a lot when they don't learn to ride—not to mention the good experience of learning to care for an animal. It teaches responsibility. If you come out to the ranch next week, I'll give you a chance to do some riding."

Crystal turned her attention back to Mr. Kirkland. "Really? That's great. But I'm not sure how long we'll be around. Maybe you could give your talk about kids and horses to my dad, if you get a chance to meet him. It might mean a lot, coming from someone like you. I mean, it sure couldn't hurt."

Mr. Kirkland yelled as the next event began. Crystal spied Shawn's camera lying close by. She picked it up and used the telescopic lens like a telescope. Nothing seemed out of the ordinary on the platform. She searched the crowd for Megan and Shawn.

Mr. Kirkland calmed down enough to say, "You give me ten minutes with your daddy. I'll have him buying a horse for every member of the family." He added, "And here come the chili carriers."

Shawn juggled three large bowls, and Megan carried the drinks. "Mr. Kirkland," Shawn said, "I'm sorry. We forgot to ask if you wanted anything. I'd be glad to go back."

"Don't worry about me, son. Thanks. You go right ahead and dig into that chili. It will be a real experience." He watched them eagerly.

Crystal took a big bite. "Are you sure this is the hot kind?" she said one second, and grabbed for her drink the next. She gasped for breath. "Wooee, that must be the hottest chili in Idaho."

Kirkland roared with delight. "I don't know about that, little lady, but it sure is the hottest chili in Lewis County."

"That's what they told us down there," Megan said. She took one small precautionary bite.

Crystal made no more comments as she ate the chili. She didn't want to give Mr. Kirkland the satisfaction of knowing a California girl couldn't handle it. She sensed his watching her every movement. She tried to sip her drink, but it was gone before she finished a third of the chili.

"It doesn't matter," she told herself. "If I said I like hot stuff, then I'll eat hot stuff. Besides, the discomfort's only temporary."

She took another heaping spoonful and shoved it into her mouth. Tears welled up in her eyes, and her nose began to run. She didn't bother explaining. She jumped up and ran for the concession stand, still carrying the half-empty bowl.

Three large drinks later, she bought extra drinks for the others and returned to the booth, sucking on a piece of ice. "Did you see anything yet? Down at the platform?"

"Haven't been watching that much. Except, I did notice that Suzy Ann's getting a little sunburned," Shawn answered.

"That's what she gets for wearing a dress like that," Megan retorted.

"Sure wish we knew what's happening back in town," Shawn said quietly.

Kirkland expounded the details of saddle bronc

riding. "This is like the bareback event, but the cowboy uses a saddle, halter, and one rein. Notice that he can only hold on with one hand. He has to spur the horse and stay on ten seconds. That old boy out there is one of the best. He's out of Billings, Montana. He's got a chance at the All-around Cowboy Award."

"Crystal!" Megan said under her breath. "Look through this lens. Isn't that the stagecoach right behind the committee's stand?"

She adjusted the lens focus. "Hey, it is! Shawn, look down there!"

"Hey, great!" he said. "Let's go down and get some pictures before the committee rides off. I want one of me sitting on top."

Kirkland whooped beside them. "There he goes! That's the best calf roper you'll ever find. Did you see how he threw that calf to the ground? Now he's got to tie three of its four feet. A champion like Bob can do it in less than ten seconds."

"Let's go now," Crystal suggested.

"Right after this event," Shawn paused.

Crystal turned to the roping exhibition. She remembered that was one of Shawn's skills. She studied the precision of the lead rider, contestant, and horse. She was impressed that the animal knew just the right time to cut, to turn, to halt. The cowboy threw the calf down and tied three of its feet in seconds. "Is your horse like theirs?" Crystal asked.

"Sure is," Shawn told her. "His name is Spade.

108

I've had him since the day he was born, nearly eight years ago. I green broke him myself."

Megan nudged Crystal. "Why don't we sneak back to town and see what's going on? This rodeo stuff's not my style anyway."

"Shawn wants a picture of that stagecoach first. Maybe after that, we can talk him into it."

Mr. Kirkland slapped his hat across his knee again. "OOOEEEE! Would you look at that boy go? Kids, that stunt was dreamed up by Bill Pickett down in Texas. We call this bulldoggin', though it looks like steer wrestling. A perfect plunge from a speeding horse to the neck of that running steer. Can't beat that for pure drama, hey?"

Crystal looked at Shawn and he cleared his throat. "Mr. Kirkland, sir? We'll be seeing you. We'd like to get a closer look at the stagecoach. Thanks so much for letting us . . ."

"What? You aren't going to miss the main event, are you?" Kirkland exclaimed.

Crystal asked, "Oh? What's that?"

"The official, one and only, Kamiah Pioneer Days Suicide Run." His dark eyes flashed.

"It has to do with the Nez Perce Indian war," Shawn added. "You ever heard of Chief Joseph?"

The girls nodded. "From my dad," Crystal explained.

Mr. Kirkland picked up the story. "Yep, Captain Perry of the U.S. Army got beat bad in one of the early battles near Whitebird. Surrounded by Indians, he sent word to Mt. Idaho for reinforcements.

109

Seventeen men tried to break through. They barely made it. We call it the 'Charge of the Brave Seventeen.' That was on July 5th, 1877. We don't forget it. The last event's an endurance race that commemorates the charge. See this buckle? Genuine Idaho silver. I won the Suicide back in '36 and '37. Worth a bundle today."

Crystal focused her full attention on the rancher. "Silver? Are all the awards in silver?"

Kirkland looked pleased. "We try to make it worthwhile. We pay them in genuine silver. The All-around Cowboy's prize is worth $10,000. They bring the silver from Kellogg, direct from the smelter."

Questions flew like bullets from the three: "Where's the silver now?" "Is it well protected?" "When do you give it out?"

"Whoa, don't you kids worry. We've got an armored car from Spokane guarding it. In fact, it's right next to the stagecoach now. They watch it like hawks."

Crystal grabbed Shawn's camera from Megan and peered through the lens. "That must be what they're after," she surmised quietly.

Megan squinted her eyes. "But, there's such a gang of them—that is, if we have it figured right. Surely the silver wouldn't stretch that far."

"Oh, I don't know," Crystal retorted. "It sounds like a lot to me."

"They could get a lot more than that in town," Shawn commented. "I agree with Megan. It sure seems like an awful lot of trouble." He raised the lens for another look.

Crystal brushed back her hair. "Maybe you're right. Something doesn't add up somehow."

Shawn let out a shout. "Hey, the committee's leaving the platform."

Mr. Kirkland glanced at his watch. "It's a bit early for them to ride the coach to Snowcap Butte. They act as referees from there for the Suicide Run. When the race is over, they ride back down the center of the arena, announce the winners, and give out the prizes." He put his hat on. "You know, it wouldn't hurt for me to go down and check things out before they leave. You kids coming?"

Kirkland's invitation didn't need repeating. The three were off and running.

9

THE CHARGE OF
THE BRAVE FIVE

JUST AS THEY REACHED THE STANDS BEHIND THE
platform, the stagecoach whizzed away in a
cloud of dust. Kirkland gaped, swallowed, and
said, "Well, I'll be. What's the big hurry?" He
glanced up at the now-empty dignitaries' stand.
"Surely someone could have sent a message to me.
I'm supposed to announce the Suicide Run."

Crystal walked around the armored truck. "Mr.
Kirkland, I don't see any guards around."

He hurried to the truck and peered inside the
cab. "I suppose they could be with the stagecoach.
They talked about loading the silver into it."

Crystal jumped up and tried to peek into the
small rear windows. "Shawn," she called, "can
you see in there? I think I heard something."

He shaded his eyes against the glass. "You sure
did. It's full of bodies in there."

Shawn and Mr. Kirkland tried the handles and
latches on the heavy bulletproof door. It was tightly closed, but not locked. The four stared in amazement as the door swung open. Inside the entire
rodeo committee, plus two security guards, were
crammed into tight quarters, gagged, and tied.

Mr. Kirkland, followed by the others, began to help the people slide out and to untie their hands and feet. As the grey duct tape was gently pulled from the victims' mouths, they began to shout.

Just then the loudspeaker called for Mr. Kirkland to come to the announcer's booth. Kirkland sent Shawn to tell them he'd be there as soon as he could. Meanwhile, they tried to make sense out of the distraught crew who climbed out of the truck. They quieted everyone, and signaled one of the guards to speak first.

He introduced himself as Al. "A fellow approached the cab and rapped on the door. Said he was the mayor. Looked like him, too. He claimed the committee wanted a few publicity shots for TV. He asked if we minded if he and the rodeo queen posed by the silver. After all, I says to myself, it's their silver."

The other guard, Fletcher, continued the story. His face flushed in anger. "Then, some dame with a camera has a powder puff—says she wants to dust off our faces, something about glare on the camera. The next thing we know we wake up in the back of the truck, with people piled on top of us."

Charlie Oh stomped his foot. "I knew that other Chinese fellow was up to no good. As soon as we got a message that it was time for us to go, we ran right into the strangest gang. Everyone of them looked like us—impostors!"

"Cheap imitations," sniffed Suzy Ann. "She couldn't be elected queen of Slickpoo."

Kirkland snapped to attention. "Now that you're untied, we've got to chase after that coach. They can't have that silver."

"Forget the silver," Fletcher snorted. "We've got to get that gold."

"GOLD!" a chorus echoed halfway across the stadium.

"That's right. We received a call this morning while we were picking up your silver in Kellogg," Al explained. "We were ordered over to Elk City. They opened an old shaft and fixed up the smelter last spring when the prices shot so high. The whole thing was kept quiet, so's the place wouldn't be invaded by weekend prospectors. This was their first shipment. We were supposed to drive it on to Butte this afternoon."

Kirkland wiped his forehead and neck with his green bandana. "How much gold was there?"

"It was in gold buttons," Al stated.

"What?" Crystal asked, puzzled.

"They were round gold buttons that had only been partially refined," Al explained. "Still, there must have been several hundred pounds. Fletcher and I figured it to be worth over a million bucks."

"A million dollars!" Megan exclaimed. "I believe we've found what they've been after all along."

Kirkland's neck turned crimson. "So, they made fools of us. But, we can't just stand here gabbing."

Shawn ran up at that moment and shouted, "I found a man tied up inside one of those metal trashbins behind the stands."

Several of the men rushed to where Shawn pointed and pulled out a disheveled, kicking, aging cowboy. They pulled the tape from his mouth and untied him. "I'll kill them," he threatened. "That's what I'll do. They can't put one over on Tommie Baxter and get away with it."

"Okay, Tommie," Kirkland said. "Settle down. Let's get our bearings. We can't do anything until we know where we're going."

Kirkland turned to the kids. "Tommie used to be our rodeo star. He owns the stagecoach."

"It cost me $80,000. I ain't gonna let no copycat cowboy steal it from under me. I'll . . ."

Kirkland shouted orders like a general. "You guards! Get your rifles and follow me. We'll grab some horses, and . . ."

"We can't ride no horses," Fletcher interrupted.

"Why not?" Kirkland exploded.

"Company rules," explained Al. "If we get in trouble, we've got to call the Spokane office immediately. No pursuit allowed."

"I tried to tell them," Fletcher complained. "As soon as they called off those state patrol guys this afternoon, I knew big trouble was brewing."

Now Crystal's mind really clicked. All those antics in town were a diversion away from the rodeo grounds and the armored truck. These aren't your run-of-the-mill thieves, Crystal thought. They're smart and creative, I've got to admit.

"Okay, let's get moving. How many of you fine people, besides Tommie, know how to ride hard horseback?" Kirkland asked with a scowl. Only Shawn raised his hand.

"Look, Kirkland," the mayor blustered, "That's law business. I don't think we should . . ."

"Well, the Suicide Run's my business," Kirkland countered. "So I guess that leaves Tommie, the kid, and me."

"The mayor's right," Charlie Oh cautioned. "Those people are armed. Besides, we've still got to judge the Suicide Run. Everyone is waiting."

"I sure would like to ride," Suzy Ann said in a wistful way.

"Dressed like that?" Mr. Kirkland roared. "No way!"

"Mr. Kirkland, Megan and I can help," Crystal offered in her most grown-up voice.

Kirkland pounded his fist in his palm in exasperation. "Two old men and some kids? We haven't got a prayer."

"We do have that much," Shawn quietly added.

"That's what they said when the charge left Mt. Idaho," Tommie Baxter challenged.

Kirkland maintained his command of the situation. "Tommie, you and I will ride hard . . ."

Shawn interrupted, "What about us? You're going to need more help."

"I may need two of you," he barked. Kirkland grabbed the guards' rifles and handed one to Tommie. "You won't be needing these in a phone booth," he scoffed. Fletcher and Al glowered, but they didn't bother to protest.

"Son," Kirkland said as he motioned, "you put

that little dark-haired gal on a horse behind you. We'll see if you can keep up. Tommie and I know a shortcut, so maybe we can get ahead of them."

"No," Crystal cried to herself. "Not Megan, me! I'm the one who's supposed to ride behind Shawn and be in on the capture." But she stood there, saying nothing.

Mr. Kirkland turned to Crystal. "You have ridden a horse before, haven't you?"

"Well, sort of, that is, I think so. . . ." Crystal wondered what she was getting into.

Kirkland waved his hands as he talked. "You don't have to be a pro for what I'm thinking. Tied up to the back of that long blue trailer over there is a gray Appy, all saddled. He's gentle as can be. Mount him and head over to the meadow. Call Sergeant Kingman from the farmhouse you come to. Tell him to bring the state patrol and meet you at County Road 19. Just follow the Old Pioneer Trail until it hits the highway. He'll know what you mean."

Crystal's heart jumped at this prospect.

"Then, hustle up there to meet them," Kirkland continued. "If you're not sure of your direction, just give the Appy his lead. He'll go right for it. Bring them back down that trail until you catch up with us. Maybe we can run into those guys before they escape by the highway."

Crystal nodded, though she felt a little faint. She turned to run.

"Be careful, Crystal," Megan called after her.

"I will," Crystal answered back, and then added on impulse, "and pray for me. I'll pray for you, too." She took a deep breath to overcome the stiffness she already sensed in her limbs.

Kirkland led the charge into the arena. They headed for the long string of horses standing in place for the Suicide Run. Crystal dashed for the trailer. She could hear the rodeo announcer say, "Folks, let me draw your attention to the top of Snowcap Butte. The stagecoach with the official committee's now approaching. All racers must wait for the gun or be disqualified."

She heard some kind of squawking, and then, "Could someone please tell me who those four on the field are? I don't have them listed on the roster. Hey, what's going on?"

Crystal easily found the horse tied to the blue trailer. She freed him and stood staring at him for a moment. She tried to remember how to get into the saddle. She knew to put her foot in a stirrup, but which side? And how would she get her foot that high without help?"

She placed her left foot in the stirrup. But this threw her whole body backwards. She couldn't reach the saddle to pull herself up. The big horse just turned and stared at her.

She clutched the reins and led the horse to the side of the trailer next to the tire fender. By standing on the fender she reached both the stirrup and saddle horn. She pulled herself on top of the large gelding.

"Okay, go!" she shouted. She held on to the saddle horn, but the animal didn't budge. "Giddyup! Come on . . . *please.*" she pleaded. He stood still.

Cautiously she reached back and gently patted the horse's rear. That didn't faze him. Disgusted, she slapped her thigh, which caused her leg to kick the horse in the side. He trotted forward. Crystal gripped the saddle horn with both hands.

As she accustomed herself to the animal's movements, she relaxed and held the reins. She recalled Patty telling her that you guide a horse by pulling the reins to the left or right. She pulled left. The horse moved that direction. "It works!" she cried. "I can ride!"

She remembered her task. She kicked the horse once, then twice. He speeded up. She felt the saddle leather pound up and down beneath her.

Crystal negotiated her way out of the parking lot and down the road to the meadow. A police car turned off the highway toward her. She coaxed the horse out into the middle of the road and tried to flag the car down.

As the driver slammed on his brakes, dust and gravel flew. The sudden noise frightened the otherwise peaceful horse. He reared and threw his head back. Crystal envisioned herself thrown to the road, back broken, and paralyzed for life. But her grip held. The horse quickly settled down.

Sergeant Kingman got out of the car. She caught her breath and talked fast. "The impostors stole the silver and gold. Mr. Kirkland says you've got to stop them on the Old Pioneer Trail. So hurry—"

"Whoa, young lady. Come again?"

She tried to slow down. "That gang of people we've been suspecting stole the stagecoach. They tied up the rodeo committee and the armored car guards. They robbed the guards of a million dollars worth of gold buttons. Mr. Kirkland chased after them, but he wants you to head them off at Highway 19. I'm supposed to go with you," she concluded.

"I'll head them off, all right," Kingman declared, "but you stay here! And try to keep that horse out of the middle of the road." The sergeant spun his car around and streaked back to the highway.

Crystal was tempted to follow him. But she knew that would upset him, and maybe slow the action. She turned the horse around, kicked him, and decided to follow the stagecoach's path. As she gained confidence she discovered she needed only one hand to hold the saddle horn. However, the bouncing hurt her bottom.

"I'll never catch them," she moaned to the gray-spotted horse. "I'll be the only one to miss everything." In desperation she steered the horse across a small meadow toward a stand of pines. "I'll have to find my own shortcut somehow!" she told the animal.

For several breathless moments she held on tight as the Appaloosa trotted faster. He seemed to know his way through the trees, boulders, and fallen logs. Then, the woods suddenly stopped. Straight ahead of them was a sheer drop-off.

Crystal jerked back on the reins. The horse halted in an instant, throwing her out of the saddle as she clung to his neck. He eyed her as she slid back into the saddle. She surveyed their situation.

They stood on a cliff that overlooked a small creek. Crystal gasped in amazement at what she saw. Beside the creek she spied the stagecoach, stalled. That was the good news. The bad news was, no way could she dare ride the horse down that sheer incline. All she could do was sit and stare. She strained her ears as she thought she heard some voices. The words of the fleeing robbers carried up the cliff.

"I told you we should drive out the front gate instead of traipsing down this forsaken rock bed!" one of them shouted.

"No use taking a chance on meeting the law coming down that tiny one-lane road. This way we're out of town before any of the local yokels know what hit them. With Wally and Teresa waiting in the van, we'll be in Canada before midnight."

Crystal could see a man in a black hat leaving the stage. He stopped as a girl's shrieks pierced the air. He yelled at the driver, "What in blazes is that?" He twisted around to look toward the creek.

Crystal scanned the creek, too. She thought she recognized the voice. "Help! Please help! I think he's broken his neck." It was Megan.

Now Crystal could see Shawn. He was sprawled awkwardly across the creek, face half in, half out of the water. He and Megan blocked the stage's path. Megan leaned over him. She held the horse's rein in one hand.

Crystal felt nausea rising as she watched from the bluff, helpless. "Lord, help him!" she prayed. "Something's gone terribly wrong."

"Boss," the driver called, "the kid's had an accident. Looks bad. And they're right in our way."

"Drive around them. Keep this rig moving, you idiot," the man with the black hat ordered.

"Can't, boss," the driver insisted. "Too many boulders to cross anywhere but right where they landed. Besides, I don't know how to run this thing to the side," he admitted.

"I thought you said you knew how to . . ." the leader shouted.

"I promised to get it going, and stop it. I sure didn't claim to turn it on a dime."

The man with the black hat yanked open the stagecoach door. "Everybody out! Get those kids out of the creek. Darrell, you stay here and drive it across when it's clear. We'll reload on the other side."

Two of the larger men, one dressed like the mayor and the other like the banker, attempted to pick up Shawn. "My back! My neck! You're killing me," he bellowed. They dropped him back in the water. Megan cried louder than ever.

Crystal's eyes filled. "This is no fun, Lord," she

prayed. "It's supposed to be like a game, with nobody hurt, certainly not Shawn. I've got to do something. Please, Lord, don't let me freeze. Please, Lord."

The leader pulled out a gun. "Get that horse and girl out of here. Tie them up to one of the cottonwoods. Sissy, you and Fran help with the girl."

Megan kicked and yelled and apparently bit an arm or two as they dragged her to the trees. "Now," the leader commanded, "carry the boy out, or we'll run the stage right over him."

Shawn screamed in agony as they lifted him. They lugged him to the meadow and tumbled him on the grass. Megan managed to escape, and rushed to his side.

The masquerade party stood in line as Darrel drove the stage across the creek. Two of them held guns on Megan and Shawn. Crystal was crying so much she thought at first she just imagined a movement behind them. She wiped her eyes and could see two more men. They seemed to be prowling low behind the others. Then it dawned on her. "All right!" she whispered as she recognized Mr. Kirkland and Tommie Baxter.

Before the gang realized what had happened, Mr. Kirkland's rifle was resting on the leader's head. "One move and there won't be anything left of your body above the shirt collar," he growled.

Tommie snarled, wild with rage, "All of you, on the ground, facedown. No jury in Idaho would convict me if I shot you all."

123

Then Shawn rose up from the grass and shook himself off. He tried to wring the water from his clothes. Megan hugged him. "We did it! We did it!" she whooped. Crystal gasped as they danced around the meadow.

She slowly heaved a big sigh of relief. "Sooo, they planned a skit of their own all along."

All of a sudden, one of the men tried to escape. He sprinted toward the cottonwoods. Kirkland and Tommie stood motionless with their guns on the others. Shawn dove for the feet of the fleeing suspect. It was a good tackle. They both landed in the creek, with Shawn on top. He pinned the man's arm behind his back.

"That-a-boy," Tommie yelled. "Kirkland, these kids are okay."

"Hey, watch the stagecoach!" Megan shouted.

The driver had hit the reins, and started the horses. "Hold your gun, Tommie," Kirkland cautioned. "We'll leave him to the sheriff."

"But he's got the gold," Megan protested.

"And my stagecoach!" Tommie grumbled.

Crystal sensed it was time to act. All the others had done their part, now she would. "I've got to do it. I'm going to do it. Please help me, God," she said over and over as she kicked her heels with all her might. She clung to the saddle horn.

The gray Appaloosa stumbled over the cliff, but didn't fall. He tripped, but wouldn't quit. They slid, but not out of control. Everything blurred for Crystal. This wasn't a dream; it was frightening

124

reality. But she didn't have time to think about it. All her energies were channeled to survival.

Finally, the big gray hit the trail. Crystal jerked the reins right. All she knew was that she was going to aim towards the barreling stagecoach and try to stop it.

Before they hit the stagecoach the sturdy Appaloosa reared back on its hind feet. He kicked his front legs toward the oncoming stage. Crystal clutched the saddle horn, but this time the furious movement of the horse proved too much. She flew off his back and plummeted to the gravel roadway, right in front of the stage.

"Crystal!" she heard Megan scream in terror. She lay stunned for a moment. Then she tried to raise herself up and roll out of the way. But she couldn't move. Abruptly, just before reaching her, the stage horses stampeded to the left of the Appaloosa.

The horses attempted to climb a sandy bank. The top-heavy stage tipped wildly, and the driver leaped to the ground. The huge stagecoach crashed on its side, trapping the driver underneath.

Crystal could faintly hear the driver's groans and pleas above Shawn's voice. "Crystal! Crystal!" he cried. He bent down by her on the dirt road. She didn't make a sound.

CRYSTAL LET OUT A BREATH, SLOW AND LABORED. She mumbled something. Shawn leaned closer. His hand touched her forehead and gently swept back her hair. "What did you say?" he prompted.

"I said, 'Could I have one kiss before I go?' " She opened one eye, and couldn't help letting a grin escape.

By now, Megan had reached them. "Crystal LuAnne Blake! How can you joke at a time like this?" she scolded.

"Who's joking?" she said, as she cautiously sat up and took inventory of her wounds. A few sore muscles and one ugly scratch on her arm. "See? I'm hurt."

Megan helped Crystal limp back to the others, and Shawn led the big gray horse. Kirkland greeted her. "Did that fall bust you up, missy? Sure was a brave thing to do."

"I don't think it was the fall that busted me as much as the ride. You see, really, Mr. Kirkland, I have to be honest. That was my very first time riding."

Tommie and Mr. Kirkland glanced at each other and shook their heads. "Imagine that, Tommie, she conquered that grade her maiden voyage aboard."

"But I've read all about it," Crystal added, "and my friend, Patty, told me about everything."

"Well, I can tell you," Megan said, "it's the last time I want to ride. Nothing personal, but from now on I walk, or travel with wheels."

"What do we do now, Mr. Kirkland?" Shawn inquired.

"Just wait for Sergeant Kingman. You might as well sit down and relax. You did contact the sergeant, didn't you, missy?"

"Yes, he's coming. Boy, you guys had me worried," Crystal admitted. "From the bluff I thought you were really hurt, Shawn. And Megan, you had a class act, too. I think you ought to try out for the lead in the school play. It was very emotional."

"Oh, yeah? No kidding? So you even cried a little?" Shawn said with obvious satisfaction.

"Sure! How was I to know you were faking?"

"Well," Shawn faltered, "I got a little emotional myself. Your fall from the horse—it really scared me."

"It did?" The thought gave Crystal a warm feeling. "It scared me, too," she stammered. "But I was so intent on stopping that stagecoach that I didn't think about it too much."

They heard Kirkland shouting. He pointed his rifle down the trail at some men who walked their way. "Hey," Crystal said, "it's Sergeant Kingman, and he has some officers with him. I met him before I got a chance to call him. Then I tried to catch you by making a guess at a shortcut. Maybe the horse knew where he was going. Anyway, we wound up on that ridge."

"A good thing you did," Megan answered.

"Look, Grandpa and your dad are with them," Shawn pointed out.

The sergeant and his men corralled the prisoners, and Tommie Baxter investigated the downed driver. Then he made an inventory of his rig. "You were lucky, kid," he told Crystal.

"No," Crystal replied, "it wasn't luck. We were all praying. That's a lot different than luck."

The stage driver, though shaken, wasn't hurt. They ushered him over to his friends. Tommie got help from the state troopers to right the stagecoach. He surveyed the damage. "A front axle, a few spokes, and a little varnish. Could have been worse," he reasoned.

Kirkland looked inside the coach. "You kids want to see a million bucks?" he called. There they sat. Partially refined gold buttons, each one about the size of half a volleyball.

The troopers led the string of prisoners back to the highway. The air buzzed with excitement as everyone related their view of the day's adventures. Finally, Crystal asked Sergeant Kingman, "How did you get to the rodeo so fast? I thought I'd have to call you."

"As I told Shawn, I began to suspect a mass scale

robbery of some kind. I called a few officers and a deputy from the sheriff's office to help me watch the town. About 2:30 a silent alarm blared. A minute later another went off, then another. We hardly knew which direction to go first. When we searched, we found no sign of anyone, or anything."

"That's spooky." Megan shivered.

"Then, I spotted this gizmo." Kingman held up a small electronic box about the size of a couple matchboxes.

Crystal looked it over. "What is it? It looks like a clock of some kind."

"I'm not sure how it works," the sergeant said, "but I found it on the alarm system at the gas station. It's a type of automatic timer that's preset to trip the alarm system when no one's around. When I found another one at Charlie Oh's, I knew it was a ruse. The only trouble was, I couldn't figure what their game was, what we were being decoyed from."

"So that cavalry and Indian charade served several purposes. They scared us off so they could set up their timer. And it got your attention focused on town, instead of the rodeo," Crystal concluded.

"Yes, and we've picked up some hints that they had hoped to implicate some or all of the rodeo committee members in the theft, if they could. Of course, that's all fallen through. Mostly because of the persistence of some kids I know." He winked at them.

"Anyway," the sergeant continued, "the state boys finally told me they'd been trailing an armored truck down from Elk City that reportedly held gold."

"At that point you dropped everything and made a beeline for the rodeo grounds," Shawn offered.

"Right. But I sure hope this is the end of the line for all the games. Now no one's left in town to keep the peace," Kingman mused.

"What about the van?" Crystal asked. "I heard them talk about some others waiting for them."

The lawman filled them in. "When we arrived at the crossing, the van started to pull away. It was towing a white Jeep."

At the mention of the Jeep, the two girls glanced at each other, dumbfounded.

"They got stuck in the loose sand of the road's shoulder," Kingman continued. "After that, they didn't put up much of a fight."

Crystal asked the question they all wanted to know. "Who are these people, anyway?"

"From what we can gather so far, it's the Tankersley team from Florida. Ever hear of them?" Sergeant Kingman looked around.

Mr. Blake spoke up. "You mean the ones who travel the country with big con schemes, bilking people with wild investment ventures?"

"They're the ones. They usually stick to the large cities. Often impersonate famous people and such. I guess they're tired of the nickel-and-dime stuff and wanted to cash in on one big job. Somehow they got wind of the mines up here. Inside the van are more costumes and makeup than in a Hollywood studio."

"Dad," Crystal suggested, "this sounds like the makings of a story."

Mr. Blake shrugged. "Maybe so. But it's so incredible. Who'd believe it?"

Mr. Kirkland mounted his horse, waved goodbye, and rode back toward the arena. Shawn helped Crystal up on the big gray and then mounted his horse. He reached down his hand for Megan.

"No way!" Megan said. "Never again. That horse almost beat me to death."

They all walked back to the highway as Sergeant Kingman left a guard with Tommie and the stagecoach. Along the way, Crystal, Megan, and Shawn repeated the whole story to Mr. Blake and Rev. Sorensen. When they reached the road, Mr. Kirkland and the armored car waited for them. They could hear Kirkland and the guards arguing.

"What do you mean, company policy?" Kirkland demanded.

"We can't drive the armored truck off the road except to enter a parking lot." Fletcher was adamant.

"I don't believe this!" Kirkland shouted at near fever pitch.

"Our supervisor's driving in from Spokane," Al informed him. "We'll have to wait to hear from him what to do."

"Sergeant Kingman, you talk to these men," the

rancher insisted.

"I'm afraid this is out of my jurisdiction. If they want to leave the gold out there, it's their necks, not mine." The sergeant's eyes twinkled. "However, the folks at the rodeo deserve to know why the Suicide Run had to be canceled. You know what I mean?"

Kirkland caught on. "Why, yes. I'll have to tell them there was an attempted robbery, and now a million dollars worth of gold buttons lies out on the trail."

"Talk about Suicide Run," Crystal laughed. "In minutes that stage will be torn apart."

"Al! Get this car down the trail, and hurry!" Fletcher barked, as he hopped in without another word.

They all laughed as they watched the metal monster bump and bounce along the rocky path. A patrolman followed behind.

Crystal turned to her father and Rev. Sorensen. "And what have you two been doing all day?"

"I thought things were pretty exciting for us, until we got back here," her dad replied. "We saw some artifacts that seem to be left over from Lewis and Clark's stay here in Kamiah Valley. An ax-head and other things. The university dated them to the early 1800s. Crystal, we'll need you to take some pictures for us. I'm sorry about running off with your camera. I didn't notice it until we were ready to come back.

"Also, we met Sergeant Kingman's uncle. He

knew about the Lewis and Clark horses. Some of his Nez Perce family took care of them one year. Anyway, we've had a profitable day."

Mr. Blake pulled off his hat and ran a hand through his brown hair. "Listen, girls, Rev. Sorensen invited us over to his place for church tomorrow and Sunday dinner. I promised him we'd stop by early so you ladies could fix a dessert."

"Dad! You didn't!" Crystal's eyes implored.

"He said you gals might bake a good fruit pie," Rev. Sorensen added. "It'd be real nice to have some pretty ladies and home cooking around the house for a while."

Mr. Blake ignored Crystal's silent plea. "Then, on Monday, we'll take some pictures and be on our way."

"That reminds me," Crystal added. "We might have a whole new project for you, Dad. Someone up at Elk City is sure trying to keep something quiet with this gold mining, don't you think?"

Mr. Blake held up is hand. "I think we've had enough adventures for one trip. You girls better watch out, or I'll never get you home in one piece."

"I agree to that, Mr. Blake," Megan replied. "All I want is our motel room and a shower."

"Ah, yes," Crystal mocked, "the Kosy Korner, where rest and relaxation are the rule . . ."

"Not the exception," Megan added.

Crystal climbed down from the horse with help from Shawn. She noticed her father and Mr. Kirkland huddled in a private conversation. Crystal patted the nose of the Appaloosa. "Thanks for the riding lesson, fella. You've been a good trainer."

She led the horse over to Mr. Kirkland. The two men stopped talking as she greeted them. "Excuse me, Mr. Kirkland," Crystal said. "Does your horse have a name? I haven't known what to call him."

Mr. Kirkland's weathered face framed a broad grin. "Yes, missy, he does have a name. It's Caleb. However, it's not my horse."

Crystal's mouth flew open. "It's not? You mean I grabbed the wrong one? I thought you told me—"

"I've been talking with your daddy, like I said I would. He's agreed to let me give you girls a reward. He says if it's okay with your mother, too, you can have the horse. He's all yours."

A shiver ran up Crystal's neck. She studied her dad's face. "Is this for real? Is he kidding, Dad?"

"Mr. Kirkland's not fooling you. He's even willing to throw in the tack as well."

"Tack?"

"Yes, the saddle, bridle, and all that." The rancher explained. "I figure this way—there ought to be some prize for your help in capturing the gang. I got back my silver. Tommie's got his stage. That's all we're after. But you kids need something. So, if Megan wants a horse, too, we'll find her one. I've got a mighty fine silver buckle for Shawn."

Crystal danced all over the road, though with a slight limp. "He's mine? All mine? Caleb's mine?" She hugged the horse tightly.

Then Crystal noticed Megan didn't seem very excited. "Megan, wait until Patty finds out. We'll all have horses. We can ride together and . . ."

Megan turned to Mr. Kirkland. "I don't know how to say this, sir. I sure do thank you for the offer. But, I'm wondering, could I have a silver buckle instead, like Shawn? Do girls wear things like that, too?"

Kirkland laughed. "They sure do. No problem. A belt buckle, it is."

The big gray chose that moment to perk up his ears and whinny. "See?" Crystal said, delighted. "He even talks. Do we take him now, Dad?"

"We'll have to work out some details, first," he explained. "Little things like finding a trailer and calling your mom." He signaled for them to get into the blue pickup. The three piled in the back. Mr. Kirkland led the horses to his trailer.

As the pickup sped along, Shawn shouted in the wind, "You girls going to the talent show tonight?"

"The what?" Megan shouted back.

"Over at the Legion hall in Kamiah. It's a local talent show. You know, songs, skits, jugglers, the whole shootin' match."

Crystal looked down at her bruises. "I don't know. We could use a little peace and quiet. Besides, we wouldn't know anybody."

Shawn grinned at her. "I know one performer you'd recognize."

"Are you going to be in the talent show?" Megan asked.

"Yup," he said.

"Really?" Crystal cried, surprised. "What are you going to do?"

He looked straight ahead as he answered, "I'm a ballet dancer."

"A what?" both the girls chorused.

"Shawn Sorensen, you're kidding us! Aren't you?" Crystal implored.

He turned to each of them, grinning ear to ear. "Actually, I'm going to play my guitar and sing."

"How come you never told us you could do all that?" Crystal asked, then answered her own question. "Because we didn't ask, right?"

"Right. So, are you going?" he asked again.

"I am," Crystal said.

"In that case, you see, I'm singing a ballad. It sure would be great if I had a girl on stage with me to sing to. It might help me win first place. How about it? Do either of you have one of those frilly western dresses?"

Crystal grimaced as Megan quickly replied, "I do! The one I wore last night."

Crystal put on her best smile. Inside, she kept saying, "I'm not going to get mad. I'm not going to cry. Please, Lord."

Shawn turned to Megan, "That would be great. Here's what you'll do. Stand by some bales of hay while I sing the chorus and first two verses of 'You Are My Sunshine.' When I get to the chorus for the third time, you walk over to where I'm standing and join in singing. It'll be a knockout!"

136

"Sing? Me?" Megan wailed. "I can play clarinet. I run the mile. I can twirl a baton, and even program a computer, but I don't sing. My voice is horrible."

Shawn looked at Megan. "Couldn't you just softly hum in the background or something?"

"Hey, Crystal sings. I mean, she really sings well."

"Really? Is that right?" Shawn turned to Crystal.

"Yes, I do sing. But not out loud. That is, I've never sung solos, just in the school choir and ensembles."

"She sings good, Shawn, really. You ought to hear her in the shower."

"Megan!" protested Crystal.

"Sorry about that. Anyway, trust me. She can sing," Megan laughed.

"How about it, Crystal?" Shawn asked.

"I'll get cold feet and embarrass everybody," Crystal stalled while she thought about the idea.

"Listen, anyone who can maneuver down a cliff the way you did this afternoon is not going to blank out on a little country talent show," Shawn encouraged.

Crystal met his blue eyes. "You think so?"

He stared back without flinching. "I know it."

"Go for it, Crys," Megan urged. "Go for it."

"May I wear your western dress?" Crystal inquired.

"Okay, but I get to wear your yellow sweater,

and take first shower when we get home. Deal?" Megan reached out her hand across Shawn.

"Deal, partner." Crystal took her hand.

"You mean, partners plural," Shawn replied as he put his hand on top of theirs. They all laughed as the wind whipped their hair.

As they turned into the rodeo parking area, Crystal considered the past twenty-four hours. "Not bad for a city girl," she decided, "not bad."

For adventure, excitement, and even romance . . .
Read these Quick Fox books

CRYSTAL Books by Stephen and Janet Bly

How many fourteen-year-old girls have been chased by the cavalry, stopped a stagecoach, tried rodeo riding, and discovered buried treasure? Crystal Blake has. You never know what new adventure Crystal will find in the next chapter!

1 Crystal's Perilous Ride
2 Crystal's Solid Gold Discovery
3 Crystal's Rodeo Debut
4 Crystal's Mill Town Mystery
5 Crystal's Blizzard Trek
6 Crystal's Grand Entry

MARCIA Books by Norma Jean Lutz

Marcia Stallings has every girl's dream—her own horse! And she intends to pursue her dream of following her mother's footsteps into the show arena—no matter what the obstacles.

1 Good-bye, Beedee
2 Once Over Lightly
3 Oklahoma Summer